forever
Anna Day

a novella by
Rand Eastwood

Forever Anna Day

Cover Art & Interior Design
by Rand Eastwood

Author Website: www.randeastwood.com

ISBN-10: 1-732-6546-0-3
ISBN-13: 978-1-732-6546-0-0

A Quality Publication by

WOODLANDS
PRESS

"Love is the emblem of eternity; it confounds all notion of time; effaces all memory of a beginning, all fear of an end."

~ Madame de Staël

Forever Anna Day

Red Kelly was sitting on the side of his bed, bent over, looking at his feet, when he noticed a cockroach peering out at him from under the dresser to his left. He turned and watched as it lingered for a moment in the cover of shadow, antennae probing about silently, before it ventured out across the faded wood floor, obliviously dragging a tiny gray dust-bunny along, snagged on one of its prickly hind legs.

This was not an unusual sight; his ancient studio apartment was plagued with them—and others.

Red followed the voyaging insect as it crossed the floor in front of him, then came to an abrupt halt when it reached the bright, slanted square of sunlight cast onto the floor from the solitary window in the east wall of his tiny apartment.

There it paused for a moment, then turned and skittered toward Red along the edge of the warm yellow grid, apparently preferring to travel along the cooler, darker areas of the floor.

As Red watched it approach, the grid of sunlight suddenly dimmed, then brightened again, and he turned to the window to see a scattering of low, puffy clouds drifting swiftly across the sky, momentarily blotting out the Saturday morning sun as they dashed ahead of a line of dark storm clouds which were fast approaching from the east. Seeing the ominous darkness building on the horizon, he made a mental note to check the news on TV for any severe weather watches or warnings, then turned his attention back to his feet.

Socks.

So that's not it, as he sat back up and frowned, perplexed.

Red was seventy-nine years old—turning eighty soon—and it bothered him whenever he set out to do something, then couldn't remember what it was.

He glanced down at his lap, pulling aside one flap of his light blue sweater.

Belt.

So that's not it either, as he sighed in frustration.

He needed to hang on; show that he was all there.

"Now what in Sam Hill was I after?" he muttered to himself, running his hand through a hazard of disheveled white hair as he glanced around the room for a clue.

He removed his spectacles, rubbed his weary eyes with thumb and forefinger, then set them back. Squinting through the thick lenses, he sighed heavily; they just didn't seem to help much anymore.

Turning back to his dresser, he craned his neck, scanning the clutter atop. Then, off to one side, nearly hidden from view, he spied his watch (!!!), its shiny silver face peeking out at him from behind the haphazard discardings of his daily life.

That's right!, as he eagerly jerked himself to his feet, mildly regarding the cockroach below as it abruptly turned and scurried away, finally ridding itself of the tagalong dust-bunny just before disappearing back beneath the dresser.

Ambling stiffly to the dresser, Red retrieved his watch from among the debris, and held it to his ear.

Still ticking, as always.

He looked at the face: the second hand—a mere sliver of metal, no thicker than a hair—snapped tirelessly around the faded dial, silently pointing to each raised hash mark as if it had been chosen for something special.

Red loved that watch.

He turned it over, letting the steel link band fall out of the way—as was his ritual each and every morning, without fail—and read the worn inscription etched into the back:

Happy Birthday, Ted
Love Forever, Anna Day

You know I do, as he slipped the watch onto his wrist.

His confidence returning, he looked up and smiled at himself in the big mirror that hung rather tenuously upon the old, crumbling plaster wall above the dresser.

He was still all there.

Leaving his bespectacled, white-haired reflection smiling back at him, he turned his attention to the framed collage of photographs hanging on the wall beside the mirror.

In the center, dominating the collage and dwarfing the photos that cascaded around it, was a large black-and-white portrait of his beloved wife, Anna. A vibrant twenty-two at the time it was taken, she was as pretty as pretty could be.

Though the photo comprised no actual color, and had faded over the years, in his mind's eye he still saw the perpetual rose in her cheeks, the hint of strawberry lurking within the amazing piles of blonde hair, the amused twinkle that forever shimmered in her riveting hazel eyes.

Anna had been the woman of his dreams; his cherished

wife of forty-six years. She was the one and only woman he had ever loved, and he loved her more than anything else on God's green earth. There was no doubt in his mind that she was his soulmate, and for more than four decades she had been the centerpiece of his life.

Red's heart still ached every time he gazed upon her image.

He had inscribed a caption under her photo; a quote, originally penned by Thomas Jefferson—the Founding Father of this great nation, and one of Red's most inspirational heroes.

Jefferson, like Red, had felt a nearly incomprehensible love for his wife, Martha—whom he had affectionately nicknamed "Patty"—and had written of his love for her:

> *In every scheme of happiness, she is placed in the*
> *foreground of the picture as the principal figure.*
> *Take that away, and it is no picture for me.*

Red had never come across any other words that came so close to capturing his own love for his dear wife Anna.

"Amen brother," Red whispered, now heavy of heart.

His eyes then moved from his lovely young Anna to the rest of the photos, taking in what had once been his life, so long ago.

The next picture showed Red proudly embracing his new bride in the wedding chapel at Southern Plains Baptist, his thick red hair appearing nearly black in the old black-and-white photo. He stood proudly, handsome and distinguished-looking, with Anna adorning his arm like a glimmering jewel.

The wedding had been wonderful, had gone off without a hitch; but the reception party...now *that* was something else!

Sparing no expense, he had thrown one hell of a bash!

During his time in the army, he'd religiously socked his pay-checks away, knowing that magical day would eventually arrive—the day he would marry Anna, which would be the happiest and most long-awaited day of his life. But doing so was difficult at times; most of his buddies were blowing their pay living it up in whatever town they found themselves on the rare weekends they were given leave—booze, drugs, hookers... you name it, they did it. The war was hard; the men needed any relief they could get, any distraction, anything that could numb them of the horror, destruction, and carnage of war that they witnessed practically daily. But Red had persevered, held to his conviction. Four long, hard years he saved—and now, the war over, and Red back home, he was glad he had.

For the wedding reception party, he rented a big banquette hall in town, hired a catering service and bartender, stocked a full wet bar, and even booked a live band, *Hoot 'N Holler*, one of the best in the region. Famous for their cutting-edge renditions of the current hits, the band featured four vocalists—all young, pretty girls—accompanied by four very talented stage musicians—a guitarist, bassist, a pianist, and drummer—all of which were backed by a 12-piece jazz ensemble.

Hundreds of people had showed up—from every corner of Red's and Anna's life—and the spectacular party that ensued had the townsfolk talking for years.

That was a long, long time ago—but sometimes, to Red, it seemed like just yesterday. Standing alone in his apartment, the old man smiled, remembering. Gazing at that photo, he could almost hear the laughing...the bustle...the music...

•

The alcohol was flowing freely, and the guests were loosening up after indulging in a seemingly endless buffet of food. It was getting late, and most of the older folks—including Red's parents Ray and Nicole, and Anna's parents Roger and Dottie —had given their hugs and kisses, said their goodbyes, and taken leave of the younger crowd.

The catering service was packing up, too—but before the party could take on an air of fizzling out for the evening, the band stepped things up another notch, breaking into a raucous rendition of The Andrews Sisters' *Boogie-Woogie Bugle Boy of Company B*.

The makeshift dance floor (a tiled area on one end of the banquette hall they had purposely left clear for such activity) not only filled immediately with well-lubricated dancers, but even spilled over into the surrounding dining area. Tables and chairs were hastily moved aside to make room, and the wedding reception made its official transition to full-blown party.

Red, not being one for dancing, stood leaning against the "bar" (the banquet hall sported no actual bar, so the serving counter running along one side of the adjoining kitchen had sufficed, which was now crowded with dozens of colored bottles of various sizes, a chaos of booze that only the bartender could seem to keep track of. Behind the barkeep, an entire commercial-sized refrigerator was packed with bottled beer, wine, and champagne; and two portable keg coolers were tapped and flowing generously).

He had shed his tuxedo jacket, draping it over the back of the adjacent bar stool. His shirt collar now hung open, with his yanked-out bow tie poking up from his breast pocket, its strap dangling down the left side of his chest.

With one hand in his pants pocket and the other clutching a frosty mug of cold draft beer, the new groom was thoroughly enjoying the scene now playing out before him: the crowds of friends, family members, old schoolmates, and fellow soldiers drinking, dancing, and just having a jolly good time. This was a glorious day for him, and it pleased him to see so many of his loved ones enjoying the event just as much as he was.

It hadn't taken much champagne for Anna to let loose; she

rarely drank at all, and barely weighed a hundred pounds—so when she *did* imbibe, the effect was swift and pronounced.

The girls of *Hoot N' Holler* had spent the evening whipping the crowd into a dancing frenzy, and when they broke out with *Company C*, Anna and a throng of her girlfriends abandoned their chairs and swooped to center stage on the dance floor, half-full champagne glasses still in hand, laughing and gyrating and bumping into one another—looking at once cute, ridiculous, and lovely.

Red watched his adorable bride from afar, smiling behind his dripping stein as he anticipated the nighttime activities yet to come.

Suddenly, a slap on the back.

"Red Kelly, congratulations! She's quite a beaut, eh?" came a voice from behind, hollering over the increasingly loud music and drunken frolic.

Red turned around, his face brightening in recognition.

"Kevin Clarke!" he shouted, grinning as they gripped each other's hands in a firm shake. "Lord, what's it been? Five years?"

"Yep—since graduation day," Kevin confirmed. We left ol' Franklin High, and didn't you enlist right after that?"

"Was thinking about enlisting, but got drafted first anyway. Next thing I know, I'm in boot camp. Fort Benning, down in Georgia. Went over soon as we finished training. France, right after the invasion."

Kevin's eyes widened. "D-Day?" he asked, incredulous.

"D-Day," Red confirmed, looking off somewhere and nodding slightly as he took a swig.

"Wow...no shit...see any action?"

Red turned back to his friend: "Saw some combat the first few days, but most the fighting was already over, the Germans were in retreat. Mostly trailed along after the Third, cleaning up after Patton while he chased what was left of those damn Krauts clear across France to Paris. When it was finally over, they shipped me back stateside. Fort Bragg. Stationed there till I finished out my term. Just got out, came back home, thought I'd get married."

They both grinned.

Red took a swig, then motioned to his friend with his mug.

"What about you?"

"I was thinking of going in, too, but Dad suggested I try for officer training, rather than just enlisting as a grunt. I thought that sounded a helluva lot better than infantry—front lines, fighting in ditches—screw all that! So I took the test that summer, and was accepted into the Navy's V-12 college program. Went to California, got a BA in business at Stanford, all courtesy of Uncle Sam. Guess I was pretty lucky—time I finished, the war was pretty much over. Finished my enlistment time at Norfolk, never did see any action. Now I'm back here, working in Dad's business, take it over some day. Good thing I took his advice, huh? Ol' man's pretty smart sometimes."

"What's the business again?"

"Office supplies. Business to business. We sign up corporate accounts, then provide them with bulk supplies at a pretty substantial discount."

Red looked incredulous. "So you're telling me you have a cush office job selling office supplies to other offices?"

Kevin made a sarcastic face, feigned serious thought about Red's statement, then shrugged.

"Yeah. I guess that pretty well sums it up!"

They both laughed.

"Whaddya have?" the bartender interrupted from behind.

"Don't worry, it's all on the house!" Red hollered over the ruckus. "Whatever you want!" Leaning in, Kevin ordered a shot of bourbon and a draft beer. The barkeep nodded and turned, deftly snatching down the appropriate glassware and going to work.

Red had turned his attention back to the dance floor, admiring his bride as she enjoyed the biggest night of their life, dancing and skipping around the dance floor with the other ladies like a happy kid playing with childhood friends. He couldn't help but grin.

God, how he loved her.

"She sure is a pretty one," Kevin shouted in Red's ear.

"Yes, she is!" Red shouted back, and took another pull from his dripping mug.

Kevin picked his drinks up from the bar, and held his mug up to Red. "A toast! To the newlyweds! May you live happily ever after in wedded bliss!"

Red smiled in appreciation, and the two clinked their mugs together and drank, Kevin slipping the shot in with his other hand and a quick backward jerk of his head just before the mug reached his lips for the chase.

"Damn! Good Stuff!" he spouted, wincing as he turned and slapped the shot glass down on the bar. Taking another swig of beer, he turned back to Red. "So, tell me—where'd you meet this fine young lass of yours?"

Pausing, Red upended his mug, draining the last of the beer. He turned, set the empty down on the bar, turned back, and, sighing contentedly, returned to his complacent lean—one elbow on the countertop, one hand in his pocket—to watch the young women frolic on the dance floor.

As the bartender walked up behind them to retrieve the empties, Kevin turned to him, nodding and pointing quickly back and forth between the mug and the shot glass. The man nodded back to confirm the silent order, and Kevin gave him a thumbs-up before turning back to Red.

"You say *you* were lucky, going to college and avoiding the war," Red began, still gazing at his distant Anna. But then he turned to Kevin, who was silently nodding in agreement, and looked him straight in the eye. Kevin was instantly entranced, as Red's crystal clear blue eyes seemed to be glowing.

"But I, my friend...*I* was the lucky one..."

Anna and her friends were having a ball on the dance floor, but they were getting a little winded, and a little warm—and Anna held the opinion that sweating is not very ladylike. So when *Boogie-Woogie Bugle Boy* ended, and the band kicked into another number, she grabbed Stacey by the hand and commenced pulling her best friend and maid-of-honor off the floor and back toward their table, where more cold champagne waited to be poured.

On their way across the dance floor, Stacey grabbed another girl's hand, who in turned grabbed another's, and soon an entire linked gaggle of tipsy females were giggling their way back to the table.

The bottle went hurriedly around, the slosh of refilling half-empty glasses, the clumsy clinking of glass on glass, the happy giggling of half-drunk girls.

Stacy lit a cigarette, then leaned in close to Anna.

"I swear, he hasn't taken his eyes off you all night!" Stacey hollered over the music, giving Anna a mischievous smile.

"Now what, pray tell, do you suppose that fine-looking gentlemen has in mind for you tonight?"

All the girls laughed at this, a few stealing glances across the room at Anna's man, standing so handsomely at the bar.

"Anna—oh, my God—he's SO good-looking!" It was Jenny—a friend from school whom she'd not seen for a couple of years

—sitting across from her. She'd been chubby in school, and was even heavier now, and all evening had made no bones about the fact that she was available and looking. Again she turned and glanced back at Red, then turned back, rolling her big brown eyes dreamily.

"What a hunk. You're soooo lucky, Anna."

Several of the girls nodded, voicing their agreement.

Mary, sitting on the other side of Anna, lit a cigarette, blew the smoke behind her, held the cigarette off between two fingers of one hand, propped her elbow on the table and leaned her chin somewhat sloppily onto her other hand, and slurred, "So tell us, Anna-dear...how, exactly, did you meet such a fine specimen of manhood?"

The question was met with a girly chorus:

Tell us!

Yeah tell us!

Yes where did you meet him?

Suddenly Stacey leaned in, and piped up loudly, "What, you haven't heard the story?" She looked wide-eyed and incredulous around the entire table, taunting the girls. This sent them into another frenzy.

Heard what?

Let her tell it!

Come on, Anna, tell us!

Yeah, what happened?

Throughout the pleading, Anna sat in silence, feigning disinterest as she fanned herself with a paper plate and sipped from her glass.

Finally, a hush fell over the table, and all the girls were staring at Anna, waiting.

Letting out an exaggerated sigh, Anna finally relented.

"Okay, if you MUST know..."

The cackling began again as the girls eagerly prodded her on. Then, as they quieted down, Anna leaned forward, looked around the table, and began to speak.

"I was really lucky...if it hadn't snowed so much..."

"I met her on Christmas Eve, at church." Red continued.

"Southern Plains Baptist?" Kevin asked.

"Yep. Where we just got married."

"Good church. Been there a couple times. I like the pastor—what's his name? Johnson?"

"Close. John*stone*."

"Yeah, yeah, yeah—Johnstone. He marry you guys?"

"Yep. He's been my pastor since I was a kid."

Just then, the barkeep plopped the freshly-filled mug and shot glass on the counter behind them, and they turned and picked them up. As Red took a swig, Kevin downed the shot, slapped the empty shot glass down on the bar, then took a chase from his mug.

They both turned back, looking out across the crowded hall. Red leaned in and spoke loudly above all the ruckus.

"Anyway, I went to the Christmas Eve service, just like every year. They always held two services—an early service at six, and then a later service at eight, with refreshments served in the fellowship hall between the two. I was a senior that year, and decided to go to the earlier one, in case I wanted to go out later or one of my buddies called or something."

"Makes sense," Kevin nodded, then tipped his beer.

"Well, it was snowing like crazy that night—really coming down—so during refreshments they got on the intercom and asked for volunteers go out and shovel the sidewalks and parking lot. Me and about half-dozen other guys volunteered, and we all headed out and started shoveling. By then, the snow had tapered off to just flurries, but there must have been close to six inches of fresh snow covering everything. It was a mess..."

"It was Christmas Eve," Anna continued. "At church."

The girls gasped all around the table, with one of them whispering *how romantic!*

"They always held two Christmas Eve services, with a big refreshment break in-between. I was still in high school—sweet sixteen, as they say—and me and some of my girlfriends had volunteered to help in the kitchen with the refreshments. It was a big affair, set up in the fellowship hall, so I decided to come in during the first service to help prepare in the kitchen, then serve the refreshments, help clean up, then go to the second service at eight."

"So how did you meet him!?" Jenny interrupted impatiently, and the cackling once again commenced.

Yes, how?

Come on, tell us!

What happened?

"Well, I'm trying to get to that, if you'd all stop your cackling for five seconds!"

Laughter burst around the table, then tapered off.

"So I was serving refreshments, and while I was back in the kitchen, I heard them announce over the loudspeaker that they needed some guys to help shovel snow out in the parking lot—apparently, it had really come down during the first service. I didn't think much of it at the time, but afterward, when we were done cleaning up, I went out the rear door of the kitchen to throw some bags of trash into the dumpster behind the church. That's when I saw just how much it had snowed. The cars in the lot were totally covered. The guys were out there shoveling away, but I noticed something they were missing..."

"So me and the guys are out there shoveling our asses off, trying to make some headway before everyone started trying to leave, or coming in for the late service. I was clearing the sidewalk up by the building, working my way toward the far side, where the lot hooks around back by the fellowship hall. But when I turned the corner, I looked up, and there she was..."

"The windshields. That's what I noticed. The guys were doing a bang-up job getting the sidewalks and lot shoveled, but all the cars' windshields were covered with snow. I looked down, and noticed someone had already swept the snow off the back porch, and left the snow-covered broom out there, leaning against the wall next to the door. I looked at the broom, then out at the cars, and got an idea. I grabbed the broom, tossed the bags into the dumpster, then headed into the lot, brooming the snow off all the car windows just as fast as I could..."

"Anna? She was outside in the parking lot?"
"Yep. So I round the corner, look up, and see this cute little thing scurrying around among the cars—no coat, no hat, just a dress—sweeping the snow off the car windows just as fast as she could swing that little broom of hers. Raising quite a cloud, actually. I stopped and watched. Couldn't take my eyes off her. I was truly amazed at how hard and fast she was working, especially for as tiny as she was..."

"I had snow everywhere! In my hair, down the front of my dress, in my shoes. But I didn't care. I only cared that everyone could drive safely, be able to see once they got to their cars. So there I am, working like a girl possessed, starting in the back lot by the kitchen. But when I got up close to the main lot, where it opened up around the front of the church, I looked up, and

there he was...standing there on the sidewalk, all tall and hand-
some-like, staring at me with the most beautiful blue eyes I've
ever seen. And that hair. That gorgeous mess of beautiful red
hair, sparkling with snow and ice, like he had walked right out
of a dream or something..."

"She was working away, and as she finished with the outer
row of cars and headed toward the row up close to the building, the cars parked right in front of me, she glanced up in my
direction, then did a double-take, stopping dead in her tracks.
Now granted, the back lot wasn't lit too well, and she was a
good car-length away, but when she stopped and looked up at
me, her cheeks flushed pink, her hazel eyes gleaming out at me
from under all that lovely, snow-laden blonde hair, and then
she smiled—the most beautiful smile I'd ever seen—well, that
was it. I was in love. And to this day, I believe the whole thing
was orchestrated by God himself. We were meant to meet
each other—she's my soulmate, if you believe in such a thing."
   With that, Red tipped the mug up, took a swig, smacked his
lips, and sighed satisfactorily.
   "Well I'll be da—" Kevin started, but the band cut him off,
kicking into a loud, fast jazz number, and they both watched as
people once again poured onto the dance floor, where they
melded into one big, writhing frolic, a drunken commotion that
would last well into the night...

   "Well, I couldn't help but smile at him—after all, he was by
far the handsomest young man I'd ever laid eyes on—"
   —she looked mischievously around the table—
   "—and I'd laid eyes on plenty of men, believe you me—"
   —the girls all giggled—
   "—and when he leaned on his shovel and smiled back, I

knew it right then and there. This was the one. My soulmate. The Good Lord saw fit to drop him right into my lap, and on Christmas Eve no less! Best Christmas present *I* ever got, let me tell you!"

The girls broke into a chorus of giggling and commentary, but Stacey interrupted, raising her glass to toast.

"To Red and Anna! May they live happily ever after!"

Glasses clinked around the table, then tipped. As the bottle went round again, the band broke into a loud and fast jazz number, once again stoking up the party. The girl's shouting dissolved into an indistinct din as groups of revelers surged past them and out onto the dance floor, where they melded into one big, writhing frolic, a drunken commotion that would last well into the night...

•

Back in his apartment, Red was smiling—but then his smile quickly faded, along with the memory.

Forcing his eyes from the wedding photo, he moved to the one below it: an old, yellowed Polaroid of Max, his faithful golden retriever and staunch hunting and fishing partner.

Thinking back to the night of that fateful fishing expedition, he could almost smell the campfire, hear his dog's barking as it pierced the chilled night air...

•

The barking seemed distant at first; far away, out on the edges of his thoughts, his fleeting dreams. They gradually grew louder—and, it seemed, more insistent. Then, suddenly, it was close—right next to him, as if the dog had miraculously leaped to him from twenty or thirty feet away in a single bound—and Red came out of his deep slumber and snapped his eyes open, realizing with a jolt of adrenaline that something was wrong.

The night was cold, the sky black. The enormous moon and

millions of tiny, distant pinpricks of starlight that had bathed the previous nights in a dim, cool glow had vanished, veiled behind a solid blanket of clouds that had moved in earlier that day, painting the night sky in a deep, almost palpable darkness.

During the day, the overcast sky was good for fishing, yes—but it also prompted a noticeable drop in temperatures, making for a chilly day and even colder night.

Lying on his back, Red remained motionless in his sleeping bag, moving only his eyes as he glanced around, trying to assess the commotion that had startled him awake. The tiny flames of the nearby campfire, having burned down through the night, provided little light in the near total darkness, making it even more difficult for him to determine what was happening.

But soon enough, he got the picture:

Max was standing midway down his sleeping bag, barking furiously. His front paws pushed into Red's right hip, and he could feel them nudging him mildly with each of the dog's lunging barks.

The old Retriever's head protruded out over Red's torso, the dog's attention focused on something to Red's left as he sounded his alarm, deep growls fueling his rampant barking.

Now, perhaps by the light of day, Max would strike you as just an old, weary dog, napping and hobbling his way through the last of his days; but right now—standing his ground in the darkness—he sounded every bit as threatening as any young, stout guard dog.

Ever so slowly, holding the rest of his body as still as possible, Red turned his head to his left. At first, all he could see was the dying campfire, its orange glow radiating from a smoldering layer of black charred wood and silver ashes. Then, as his eyes began adjusting to the darkness—he saw it.

It was right there!

Sitting within the short distance between his sleeping bag and the campfire, not two feet from Red, was the unmistakable vertical coil of a big rattlesnake. As if on cue, its rattle sounded, clean and brisk, as Red's eyes widened and his heart quickened and Max upped the tempo and volume of his barking.

As he squinted into the darkness, there was just enough light from the dying flames to cast the snake with a golden glow, and its criss-crossed markings materialized before his eyes—and Red immediately identified it: Diamondback, which he knew to be one of the deadliest snakes in North America.

His stomach tightened.

But he also knew that even though Diamondbacks are very dangerous, they rarely attack humans unless provoked or agitated, or otherwise feel threatened in some way.

So that meant that Max's barking frenzy wasn't helping the situation; if anything, it was exacerbating it.

Another crisp warning rattle pierced the darkness.

Without moving, Red spoke quietly to his dog. "Shhhh, boy. It's okay, Max, calm down..."

But the dog would have none of it; he was in the throes of the situation, and doing what he was born to do—protect his master—and Red's calming words did nothing to abate the dog's fury and excitement.

Red glanced around, again without moving a muscle. To his right, leaning with his fishing rod against a nearby tree, was his rifle. Although this was technically a fishing expedition, Red never ventured into the wild without his trusty firearm.

Just in case.

But it was too far away; he would never reach it without risking the quick and deadly strike of the rattler—especially with the snake already coiled high, ready to strike

Max began leaping right to left on his front paws, barking at a feverish pitch now, the snake answering in turn with nearly non-stop rattling.

Red knew he was running out of time.

Moving his eyes to up to his right, they came to rest on his hatchet, lying next to a small pile of kindling he had chopped and gathered for the campfire.

It was easily within reaching distance of where he lay.

Perfect.

Moving as gently as he could, he slid his right arm out of his sleeping bag, along the ground, keeping it low in the grass, until it bumped against the cold, dew-laden wood handle. Gripping it firmly, he shifted his eyes back to the coiled rattler to his left, took in a deep breath, and gathered all his muscles for a quick—and, he hoped, deadly—swing.

It all happened quickly, like an explosion: barking wildly, Max suddenly lunged just a little too close to the snake, the Diamondback launched itself over Red like a huge four-foot spring, and Red bolted upright, swinging the hatchet as hard and fast as he could.

Max jerked himself to the side—and a younger, more agile dog may have dodged the strike—but the old dog wasn't quite quick enough, and the snake buried its fangs deep into his left shoulder, prompting a high-pitched yelp just as Red's hatchet met the side of the snake, knocking it free of the dog as quickly as it had struck him. It sailed a few feet toward the end of Red's sleeping bag and landed in the taller grass there, writhing and swirling about—but immediately gathered itself and recoiled for another strike.

Regaining his footing, Max turned and again lunged toward the snake, deaf to Red's desperately cried "NO MAX!", and the snake shot out and this time hit its mark, burying its fangs into the soft underside of the dog's neck, again prompting a yelp from the big dog as he lurched backward.

Red was up and swinging now, this time coming down hard in the middle of the snake, cutting it cleanly in two. The back half flipped away, swirling and jerking in the grass, and Max began yelping as he shook himself rigorously, swinging the attached half-snake all around like a frayed piece of rope, attempting to dislodge it from his neck.

Red kicked out at his dog, striking him square on his shoulder and shoving him violently over and onto the ground. Pinning the scampering and confused animal down with his foot, he swung the hatchet golf-club style, striking the head of the rattler with the back of the hatchet and sending the remaining half of it into the grass, writhing and twisting.

With one leap Red was on it, swinging and swinging and swinging, until the deadly rattler was reduced to a patchwork of motionless pieces scattered about in the grass.

Finished, breathing hard, he turned to his old friend, who also lay in the grass now, shivering and whimpering. He could see, by the faint glow of the fire, that the dog's eyes were quickly glazing over.

He rekindled the fire until it was roaring, and threw every piece of that snake into it, then sat and watched them curl into ashes, popping and hissing and smoking like the evil that they were, while he cradled his beloved dog's head his lap, gently caressing him as he stared into the flames.

It didn't take long for the lethal venom to do its work; tears welled up in Red's eyes when he looked down at Max and realized he was no longer staring into the fire, but just staring.

He wept all night, clutching Max's head in his lap. At first light, he packed up his things, feeling very sad and alone...

•

Red reached up with one finger and touched the back of

dog's head in the photograph, then ran it along his back in a petting gesture.

"I sure miss ya, Max ol' buddy," he whispered.

His eyes then traveled to the right, resting on a portrait of himself in full military dress. Thinking back, he could almost hear the crunching of hundreds of boots along broken roads, across gravel drives and vacant lots, through rocky, weed-ridden fields in Occupied France...

•

Red was sore all over, and hungry as hell. His legs ached, his feet were blistered, and he was exhausted nearly to the point of dropping right there in the road.

Yesterday his unit had arrived at the town of Argentan, which now more resembled a burning pile of rubble than an actual town. Only days earlier, General Patton and the Third Army had blasted their way through Germany's 9th Panzer and 2nd SS Panzer Divisions there. The intense battle against the German stronghold had lasted eight long days, and had heavily damaged much of the town in the process. Patton and the Third had since moved on, racing toward Saint-Mihiel, Châlons, and Commercy in pursuit of the retreating Germans, and leaving what was left of Argentan in smoldering ruins.

Red's platoon had spent the entire day and much of the night helping the newly-liberated townsfolk dig out and re-cover from the ruins of war. The experience had prompted mixed emotions; even though there really wasn't much they could do for these devastated people, which was disheartening —they were, nonetheless, eternally grateful to the American troops, constantly thanking them and celebrating their mere presence—and that, at least, lifted his spirits a little.

After working late into the night, the following morning at daybreak his platoon had departed the devastated town and trudged eastward toward the tiny village of Le Merlerault, a distance of just over twenty-one kilometers.

The seemingly endless raised hedgerows that crisscrossed much of the countryside between the towns were difficult to traverse, and dangerous as well; warnings of German land mines buried in the common pathways—along with the all-too-frequent reports of the resulting demise of their fellow troops—had trickled down from the front lines, making them wary and edgy as they cautiously skirted around the small battlefields, many of which were now strewn with rotting corpses.

So they tried to keep mostly to the road during their arduous trek, though it had been heavily damaged by artillery fire, and yesterday's torrential rain had turned much of it into a muddy mess. And, the occasional sniper—heard, but never seen, and often speculated to be distant friendly fire, but they never knew for sure—had more than once driven them off the road and into the brush, ditches, and sparse woods, any cover they could manage to find, which made their journey ever more difficult and time-consuming.

And on top of all that, the men were exhausted nearly to the point of collapse.

As nightfall approached, they reached the eastern outskirts of Le Merlerault, and found the small village for the most part vacant. The Nazis had left little behind.

It is said that any day that you don't lose someone in your platoon—well, that's a good day. And if that's the case, then Red's platoon was finishing their second good day in a row.

Yesterday, during their stay in Argentan, they had suffered no casualties; but even as the newly-liberated townsfolk were celebrating the arrival of the Americans, the occasional *pop-pop-pop* of gunfire and deep rumble of small explosions could still be heard off in the distance.

But that evening in Le Merlerault, the sounds of war had ceased altogether, the air filled instead with peaceful birdsong, which was joined by a symphony of crickets and cicadas as twilight descended. Soon thereafter the fireflies arrived, dancing to nature's music—and the world seemed, at least for a moment, sane again.

What remained of Red's platoon—some thirty or so men out of the original fifty-four, now under the command of Sergeant Mitchell—had split up and occupied a row of houses—all vacant, ransacked—that ran along a narrow country road on the western edge of town. They hurriedly set up quarters, eagerly anticipating their first solid shut-eye in days.

Red joined up with his buddy Jerry Caldwell, bunking with a half-dozen others in a house near the west end of the road. Jerry was a quiet southern lad whom Red had met in boot camp and immediately befriended, believing the young man's strength of character and unwavering integrity to be akin to his own, a kindred spirit of sorts. His father worked in the textile industry, and after the war he was slated to enter the same management training program his dad had entered years before, follow in his dad's footprints, up the corporate ladder.

Like father, like son.

However, Jerry secretly held other plans; he longed for the sea, and hoped, upon completing his service, to embark on a career in international shipping. It was his hope to someday live overseas, and enjoy an exciting and lucrative career traveling around the world.

Over the months, working side by side during their training, then fighting side by side in the war—and sharing each other's hopes, goals, and dreams throughout—Red and "JC" had become good friends, seemingly inseparable.

The group of soldiers ducked one-by-one through the open

door of the abandoned house and stood at the entry, quietly surveying the wreckage and debris strewn about the room. Deciding it would suffice, they each bedded down wherever they could find an open spot.

By nightfall, they were all sound asleep.

•

Red woke in the middle of the night, and had to pee. Sitting up, he blinked around the gloomy wreckage of the house, all the random black silhouettes of broken and upturned furniture sitting about in the darkness, like so many dead creatures—save an empty, leaning bookcase that had seemingly been brought back to life by a bright square shaft of moonlight shining upon it from a tall window on the west side of the house.

Quietly slipping on his boots, he glanced around at the rest of his sleeping comrades, lying about on the floor, or occupying the few furnishings that had remained intact. Soft snoring lifted into the air like a mild breeze as Red gently rose from the tattered upholstered chair he had nestled into for the night.

None of the vacant houses along this old country road were equipped with indoor toilets; instead, small *privies* stood in the fields behind them. These tiny, quaint outhouses were quickly commandeered by the soldiers, and were now referred to as the more masculine *latrines*.

Heading for the latrine now, Red was gingerly picking his way through and around the sleeping men, heading toward the back door, when he noticed a pile of empty bedding on the floor, against the wall next to the entry into the kitchen at the rear of the house. He remembered JC had chosen that spot—but now the blankets lay empty. Red glanced around the room again, just to be sure—but quickly determined that his friend was not there.

Probably went to the latrine too, as he tip-toed through the kitchen and quietly eased himself out the back door.

Outside, the rasp of crickets permeated the balmy night air, and an enormous moon cut a bright circle in a pitch-black sky speckled with a million stars. He stopped briefly to stretch his weary limbs, then stood peering out into the moonlit field. He quickly spotted the latrine—a sharp, inky silhouette standing off to the left, perhaps twenty yards out, just inside the rotted, piecemeal wood rail fence that ran along the border of the adjacent property.

The yard between him and the latrine was overgrown with weeds and tall grass, so Red elected to skirt the property along the back of the house to the fence line, then follow the old rail fence to the latrine, using the existing path where the overgrowth had already been trampled down by the other soldiers throughout the course of the evening.

Shoving his hands into his front pocket, he started walking along the back of the house. But just as he reached the fence line and was about to turn the corner, he heard what sounded like a short, muffled scream off in the distance—and he stopped in his tracks.

Cocking his head in the direction he thought it came from, he listened intently into the night.

Nothing but crickets.

You're imagining things, as he continued on, trudging along the fence line toward the latrine, unzipping his pants as he approached the tiny structure.

Another muffled scream again stopped him in his tracks, this time followed by the distant, indistinct sounds of a man speaking gruffly, and other men laughing.

Peering across the darkened yard, he scanned the house next door, which was the last one on this street. His eyes then traveled out across the lot behind it, to a small barn that squatted in the darkness back near the woods that marked the rear edge of the property.

The barn's double-doors hung crooked and gapped, and he could just see a faint yellow line of light glowing from between them. Were the sounds coming from that barn back there? As he studied it, wondering, another muffled cry reached his ears, confirming his suspicion: the noises he heard were definitely coming from that barn.

Quickly zipping up, he hurried back to the end of the fence, then crept along the back of the house next door. When he reached the far end, he crouched behind a tall shrub growing on the corner, then stuck his head slowly out in the direction of the barn, watching and listening in the darkness.

For a moment, all was quiet. Then, the muted sound of men laughing—brief and subdued—drifted to him from the barn, floating through the dead night air.

Something was definitely up, and his curiosity kicked into high gear. Crouching, he started quietly through the tall grass toward the barn. As he neared, he heard the sobbing again, and stopped to listen, his silhouette poised under the full moon like a statue.

Then, he heard it again. It was definitely the sound of some-one crying—and, to his amazement, it sounded like a *girl!*

He broke his stance and continued tip-toeing silently to-ward the barn, skirting a short wire fence that jutted out from the front wall, creating a small pen. Perhaps eight feet square, it likely once held chickens, but no longer; the small wire-frame door located on the front of the vacant enclosure hung forever open, bent toward the ground, overgrown with weeds. He skirted the front of the pen, stepping around the bent wire door, then turned once again toward the barn.

Nearing the barn doors, he pressed himself to the wall, hiding from the telltale moon in the shadow of the roof outcropping. He stopped there, listening, glancing around. Satisfied he had not been detected, he shimmied closer to the thin gap that ran between the massive wooden doors, where a faint yellow glow sipped through from inside, casting an elongated, flickering triangle onto the ground before him.

...a lantern?

...a candle?

Finally reaching the split between the doors, he then rolled quickly over to the other side, pressed himself against the far door, and, with his fingertips, pulled the other door open ever so slightly, as quietly as he could—and peered inside.

The first thing he saw, off to his right, sitting on a crate toward the back of the barn, was Vincent Perry. Even in the near-darkness, he was easy to recognize: his pale-white skin contrasting sharply with his thick, nearly jet-black hair, slicked straight back, his close-set, beady brown eyes peering intensely out from under a thick unibrow. Vinny was a small, wiry, big-mouth tough-talker from Jersey.

He sat smoking on an old wooden crate, sweaty and shirtless, tags dangling against his bare chest, a gray fog hanging in the air around him. A lantern hung above him from a rotted rafter, casting a pale yellow, flickering glow.

Red watched as Vinny took a drag, then tipped back a steel flask, wiped his mouth with the back of his hand, then handed it up to Matt Gordon—Gordie—who stood behind him, leaning against a wooden post. Gordie immediately raised the flask, revealing a large, round sweat stain in the armpit of his shirt, which hung unbuttoned, tags dangling upon his bare chest as well. Gordie was a farm boy from the midwest—tall, lanky, somewhat oafish; but a natural outdoorsman. And man, could he shoot. Sporting a good tan and thick, curly blonde hair, he was quite the contrast, standing there next to Perry. Without looking down, he handed the flask back to Perry then stood motionless, staring off into the other side of the barn.

Red suddenly realized that both the young men were gazing across the barn to some point beyond his field of vision, as if observing something that Red couldn't quite see; but he could tell that over on the other side of the barn, somebody else—some*thing* else—was there, just out of view.

Again, he heard a muffled cry—closer now, louder—emanate from somewhere within.

He slowly creaked the door open just a tad farther, trying to see into the far side of the barn. Pushing his head hard against the opposing, rotted wood door, he was finally, just barely, able to glimpse the rest of the scene.

Somebody was standing with his back to him, his pants in a bundle around his ankles. Red couldn't tell who it was, as the lantern hung forward of where he stood, thus casting his form as a mere silhouette, dark and unidentifiable from where Red stood. And there, beyond the man's blackened shape, was a girl, bound and gagged, lying on her back, arms and legs spread wide and tied to the four corner posts of a wooden table or bench of some kind. Her face was dirty, both blackened sides streaked white with tears.

Red froze, not believing what he was seeing. He leaned closer to the opening, squinting into the smoky darkness, trying to assure himself of what he thought he was seeing—hoping that it *wasn't* what he thought he was seeing, but knowing, in his heart and gut, that it was.

The man who stood between the girl's legs suddenly grunted and spasmed, then dropped his head with a long exhale, his entire body going slack for a moment. Then, quickly backing away, he stooped to yank up his pants, buttoning and zipping as he moved further to the left, out of Red's line of sight. Looking back to the girl, Red saw that she was bleeding, the wood surface between her gaping legs red and moist, her inner thighs spattered as well.

As he solemnly absorbed the tragic scene before him, the two soldiers who had been watching the action from across the barn began raucously clapping their hands and caterwauling.

Anger flared within him.

The ensuing rush of adrenaline gave him the courage to make his presence known, to stop this horror, this crime. Yanking the barn door the rest of the way open, he stepped inside and walked briskly toward the men, his boots clopping loudly across the hollow wooden floor.

"WHAT THE FUCK IS GOING ON HERE?" he shouted, as all three of them stopped, turned, and stared at him, their eyes wide with surprise.

As he approached, the girl looked up at him, pleading with tear-filled eyes. For the first time, he noticed that she was completely bald. Her head had been shaved—though roughly, with tiny tufts of hair remaining here and there, sprouting between the multiple scrapes and bruises that marked her dirty scalp.

"It's okay, she's one of *them*," an all-too familiar voice said calmly from the shadows to Red's left. He turned, and with astonishment now recognized the third man, the unidentified silhouette: it was Jerry Caldwell.

"What do you mean, *one of them*?" Red demanded, barely able to contain himself.

"She was fucking the Krauts, to save her own skin, to hell with everyone else," Jerry explained. "Yeah, she's French—but she's a traitor. A whore. The French people think so, too—the townsfolk call what she did *collaboration horizontal*—and once the Germans are run out, and the town is liberated, they round up girls like her, and publicly shave their heads. Then they're banished from town, as punishment for collaborating with the enemy. And *they* get off easy; the *men* who collaborate with the Germans are usually executed."

Red did recall hearing something about this yesterday, back in Argentan. *Femmes Tondue*, they called them. After shaving their heads, they heaped their hair into a pile and burned it. It was said that the stench of burning hair could be smelled for miles. Some of the accused women were beaten, too—but most of them were simply run out of town after the public shaving, which for French women was considered an act of extreme humiliation. It was all over and done with by the time his platoon had gotten into town, and the women were gone. Exiled.

The one lying here before him is the first he'd actually seen.

Jerry shrugged flippantly. "Fuckin a Kraut, makes her good as a Kraut, in my book."

"So get a mattress for the bitch!" Vinny suddenly shouted, slurring his speech badly.

"Yeah, a mattress for the bitch!" Gordie echoed, equally slurred, and the two broke into a round of drunken giggling.

"Is Sergeant Mitchell aware of what you're doing in here?" Red barked over the laughing.

"Uh...that would be a mattress for the *Boche*," an authoritative voice stated from behind Red. He turned around just as the sergeant stepped out of a dark stall in the rear of the barn, tucking in his army green shirt into his khaki pants and zipping up as he approached. A large cigar protruded from his mouth, which he removed with one hand once he had confronted Red.

"That's what they call 'em," he said to Red, motioning to the girl with a wave of the cigar. "A French bitch who fucks Germans. A mattress for the *Boche*. It's slang for German soldiers. And I'm with JC there—"

—he motioned behind Red with another wave of the cigar—

"—she fucks a Kraut, she's as good as one herself. And 'sides, we caught her in here rummaging through our supplies, eating our rations—hell, we barely got enough food as it is—and tried to get away when we caught her, bolted for the woods. But the boys here nabbed her barefoot ass before she made it that far. So she's not only a whore—fucking the *enemy,* for Christ's sake —but she's a goddam *thief* on top of that. She's lucky we didn't just put her ugly, bald ass down, like a rabid dog."

With that, he returned the cigar to his mouth and took several quick puffs, the stale smoke of the cheap cigar exploding into the air around his head.

Red was stunned. He turned back to Jerry.

"JC....?" he pleaded.

Jerry just looked away, hiding his guilt-ridden face.

Furious with his friend, Red turned back to Mitchell.

The sergeant pulled the cigar from his mouth and smiled.

"By the way, there's plenty to go around," he said, jerking his chin in the direction of the girl. Placing the cigar back, he shifted it to one side, clenching it in his teeth so he could speak without removing it.

"I mean, we don't want any trouble, or any hard feelings around here, do we boys?" He looked over at them as he spoke, and a quick chorus of *nopes* and *no-sirs* answered from around the room.

"So, maybe you should take a little dip yourself." A big grin. "Maybe then it won't seem all that bad." He chuckled quietly, then added "Hell, you might even *like* it! Betcha never fucked a French girl, have ya, Kelly?" With that, he stopped and gave Red an incredulous look. "Or have you ever even *fucked* a girl? You're not still a *virgin*, are ya private?"

The others chuckled at this.

Red could not believe what he was hearing. Whore or not—hell, *Kraut* or not—this wasn't right; this was very, very *wrong*. And Red was having nothing to do with it. The fact that his friend—or ex-friend that is, as of tonight—was involved in this atrocity was bad enough; no way he could allow himself to be dragged in as well. He turned angrily to Sargent Mitchell.

"And what do you suppose *Lieutenant Powell* will have to say about this—" but stopped short, remembering that the officer had stepped on a land mine a few days ago, as they were approaching the outskirts of Argentan, and, after nearly bleeding to death in the field, had been rushed unconscious to medical, where he'd been in critical condition since.

"Lieutenant Powell got his damn leg blowed off!" Mitchell shouted in his face, pointing down to his own leg with his cigar. "And even if he survives—which is unlikely, since I hear it took most his manhood along with his leg, that's why they couldn't get the bleeding stopped in the field—but if he does, in fact, survive—which I doubt he would even *want* to, I sure as hell wouldn't—he'll be shipped back stateside, swinging a purple heart and a crutch, stead of a leg and a dick. He sure won't be coming back to *this* hell-hole. Not now, not *ever*."

Red looked down, nodding his head in understanding.

"So until we meet up with one of the other companies—which may not even happen before we get all the way to fucking *Paris*—it's *me*."

He pointed to himself with an outstretched thumb, then poked Red in the chest with his forefinger.

"Got it, private? You're *mine*."

Then, looking up at the others, he swung his cigar in a wide circle, encompassing the room.

"You're *all* mine."

Sticking the cigar back into the corner of his mouth, he

turned and strolled slowly away from Red, hands on hips, suddenly rambling to himself and shaking his head...

"Shit...even if we catch up with Patton and the Third, it'll be days...maybe at the Seille river...they're supposed to stop there for supplies..."

Overhearing this, Red summoned as threatening a voice as he could muster, and said: "Well, then, maybe *General Patton* will be interested in your...*extra-curricular activities*."

He was now shaking in his boots, from both anger and fear. Confronting a superior officer can—usually does—carry severe penalties...*especially* in the field, where accountability is lacking at best, and tolerance of such insubordination nonexistent.

Mitchell snapped around and marched briskly back, stopping with his face mere inches from Red's. He didn't bother removing the cigar this time, clenching it his teeth so hard his jaw muscles stood out on both sides.

"Listen here, private!" he barked. "We're only staying in this little shit-hole town for one more day. Day after tomorrow, we're headin out. Planches, Sainte-Gauburge-Sainte-Colombe, L'Aigle, Verneuil-sur-Avre, Dreux...lots of towns to go before we reach Paris—*if* we even *make* it to Paris!"

He suddenly reached to his side and yanked his combat knife out of its sheath, and held it right up into Red's face, turning it slowly from side to side, the steel blade gleaming and glinting in the yellow lamplight.

As the woman sobbed quietly in the background, the sergeant lowered his voice to a near whisper, and said:

"There'll be lots of land mines tween here and there, too... and snipers...and hell, even friendly fire, been gettin that all over, so many trees and hills and hedgerows—"

—he swung his knife momentarily out and about—

"—can't see shit out there, don't even know who or what

you're shootin at half the time—"

—then brought the knife back to Red's face—

"—hate to think a fine young soldier like yourself get shot by a sniper—or, God forbid, friendly fire—and go home in a box... now that'd be a bit of bad luck, wouldn't it...*private?*"

A crazed look had overtaken the sergeant's face, his eyes wild. That look scared Red, and he realized the threat was real —and also knew he could do nothing about it.

Sulking, he looked back over to the girl, who was still pleading with him with her terrified, tear-soaked eyes. He could no longer bear to look into her eyes, could no longer bear to look into any of their eyes. So he dropped his eyes to the floor in dismay, understanding that he was helpless to do anything at all about any of this.

"Yes sir, it would," He mumbled helplessly.

"Yes sir, it would," Mitchell echoed, dropping the knife and stepping away.

"So I'd say, you wanna live to see Paris—"

—he pointed the knife at the door behind Red—

"—you get the fuck outta here, and you ain't seen shit, and you don't say shit. To *anyone.* Got it?"

"Yes sir."

Without looking up—no way in hell he could look at the girl again—or any of them, for that matter—he quietly turned and shuffled toward the door. As he stepped through it, the sergeant called after him, halting him in the doorway.

"We clear, Kelly?"

Without looking back, Red answered, "Yes sir. Crystal."

"Good. Always knew you had a good head on your shoulders, somewhere under all that red hair."

The snickering faded as Red walked away.

With a knot of anger burning in his gut and tears welling in his eyes, Red trudged across the yard toward the latrine. As he stomped his way through the weeds and overgrown grass, he listened in tortured silence as the girl's sobs faded into the night behind him.

•

The following morning, Red arose to find JC's bedding and supplies gone from the house, nothing but a small clearing on the floor where they had been.

It was their last day in the village, and, since it was for the most part abandoned, there wasn't much for them to do. So the men relaxed, took it easy. Red walked around, feeling isolated and alone, watching from afar as the others joked around, or sat and smoked, or slept under shade trees. The unmistakable aroma of marijuana drifted to him occasionally, and he caught glimpses of flasks and bottles being handed around in small huddles that had formed behind a house or within a dense copse of trees.

As the day passed, he never did see JC, or the others from the barn. He knew that the sergeant would likely be in meetings somewhere, probably wherever the radio was set up, so his absence wasn't surprising. But the others? Who knows. Probably keeping a low profile, after what they did.

But he was actually glad about their mysterious absence; he had no desire to see any of them—much less talk to any of them —ever again.

The day wore on. And then, in the late afternoon, a softball game broke out.

Somebody had found an old softball somewhere—pasty-white, dirty, plagued with divots and scuff marks—and a pick-up game came together out on the edge of town, in a vacant field between the last row of houses and an old, one-lane road, flanked on the far side by shrubs and a shallow ditch.

An old wooden post, salvaged from one of the many de-stroyed fences in the area, had been employed as a bat. A set of dusty tan chair cushions served as crude bases, placed around the field in a diamond shape, and the game was on.

In no mood for games, Red initially declined playing. But the guys insisted, and he decided maybe it'd be a good way to get his mind off things for awhile, get some exercise, have a little fun. So he finally relented, and was now playing center field, far out by the road, and Brent "Bull" Mason—nicknamed for to his massive size—was at bat.

From the east, an army personnel truck was approaching along the road, bouncing in and out of the numerous potholes and making a hell of a racket. In the back of the truck, a group of soldiers sat smoking with one hand and hanging on to the side rails for dear life with the other.

The pitch, and *whack!* Bull smacked it high and long, tossed the wood post to the ground, and began heaving toward first base. At first, Red went long, shading his eyes with one hand, trying to see the tiny black dot of a ball against the bright, late-afternoon sky. But his sprint faded to a jog, then he stopped altogether, futility setting in as the ball sailed far over his head, well beyond his reach.

As the personnel carrier lumbered by, the soldiers in the back all squinted up into the sky, watching as the ball sailed toward them.

Everyone on the field was hollering, a chaotic chorus of mixed messages—victory from the crowd behind home plate, shouts of despair from the field, and a little of both from the spectators that stood along the fence that bordered the north end of the fields by the houses.

Bull had rounded first and was huffing his way toward sec-ond, the noise from the crowd escalating as he traversed the makeshift diamond unabated.

As Red and the other two outfielders stood and watched helplessly as the ball fell from the sky way out by the road, one of the soldiers in the truck suddenly stood, stretched his arms out over the rails in front of him—and caught the ball!

Ball in hand, cigarette dangling from his lips, he raised his arms in victory, smiling ear to ear as the others guys in the truck clapped, slapped him on the back, and yucked it up.

This of course sparked an immediate argument on the field, as one side began yelling *Out! He's out!* while the other side, protesting the catch, yelled *Home run! It's a Home run!*

The arguing quickly trailed off, however, as everyone on the field realized that the truck was continuing down the road, and they were soon to be out of a ball—and thus out of a game.

As the guy with the ball shrugged his shoulders and sat down, his buddies still slapping him around, the chorus of yelling quickly transitioned to shouts at the guy in the truck to return the ball. Some of the players actually began jogging toward the road, as if to give chase.

But as the truck reached the west edge of the field, and many of the players were now cursing and trudging away, the catcher flippantly tossed the ball over his shoulder.

Just clearing the side rails behind him, it bounced along the road, rolled into the brush, and vanished out of sight just as the truck disappeared around the bend, leaving only a swirling trail of dust hovering above the road.

The shouting died down, and Red turned to his teammates. They were all looking at him. He turned back to the road, and realized he was the furthest one out—and even though it was probably some twenty or thirty yards away now, he was the closest one to the ball, which now lurking somewhere behind that line of brush. It had probably rolled into the ditch that ran along the back side of the road.

"I got it!" he hollered across the field. In the distance, he saw Bull quickly tag up at third and stand, looking confused, unsure if he should proceed to home plate. As Red turned to run in the direction of the lost ball, he heard the arguing start up again on the diamond behind him.

The sun was sinking in the sky, and dusk was setting in, giving the field, the road, and the woods beyond an almost surreal quality, still and shadowy. As he neared the brushy area just before the bend, still perhaps ten yards away, he could see through a slight opening in the brush, and as luck would have it, spotted the ball. Apparently resting on the inside edge of the ditch, it sat just below ground level. He could barely see the rounded top of it poking up, the pasty white, marked, and dirty surface glaring softly in the rapidly setting sun.

He quickened his pace, anxious to retrieve the ball and get on with the game. But as he neared—twenty feet, ten feet, closer—he began to slow, his stomach knotting up as what he was seeing came into better focus, and he slowed to a stop. Standing in the road, just this side of the brush line, he could now see that what he thought was the softball, was not; he stood, shoulders slumped, watching as several flies buzzed and landed, buzzed and landed on the shaven head of a young girl—pasty white, dirty, marked—that was lying motionless in the ditch, her naked body haphazardly covered with leaves, branches, and other debris.

He stood, blinking, heartbroken.

Then, off to his left, on the edge of the road, half-buried in leaves, he spotted the ball. Leaving the horrific scene undisturbed, he trotted over, scooped up the ball, and ran back toward the ball diamond, the crowd cheering as he reached the halfway point and heaved it into the infield.

"Play ball!" he shouted, his mind already blocking out the horror he had just witnessed.

Turns out, yesterday wasn't a good day after all...

•

Red had carried that memory with him his entire life. The horror of finding the dead girl—dirty, naked, covered in leaves and flies—was bad enough; but the *guilt* that plagued him—the inescapable feeling of responsibility for what had happened to her, the unending remorse he held deep in his heart for not having acted when he had the chance, of being too young and scared and stupid and confused to do the right thing, and as a result of his cowardice and weakness a young, innocent girl had died—was nearly unbearable.

This was the one thing—the one deep, dark secret—that he had never told anyone about, not even Anna. No, he vowed he would take this one to his grave. Meantime, he would spend the rest of his life doing his damnedest to do the right thing, no matter what the circumstances. In essence, he would be paying —and dearly so—for that one unforgivable mistake, that one error in judgement that he made as a young man—even if he *was* still a boy, just a teenager—for the rest of his life...

•

Back in his apartment, he stood for a moment, once again silently grappling with that memory, once again trying to bury it, tuck it away in the dark recesses of his mind where it would never again rear its ugly head.

And once again, he succeeded.

Mostly.

Finally tearing his eyes from his military portrait, his gaze fell to the bottom of the collage—a very, very old photo, faded, cracked, yellowed, blackening around the edges: Anna's parents, Roger and Dorothy Hart.

The dapper couple stood before a lush flower garden, the famed Annaday Bed & Breakfast looming in the background. Married in the spring of 1927, they had honeymooned in New Zealand, staying at Annaday in the suburbs of Wellington on the recommendation of friends.

The young couple quickly fell in love with the large, luxurious house that stood on Tinakori Hill, overlooking both the city and the harbor. The sightseeing was phenomenal, as the hotel was situated near the Houses of Parliament and several embassies, as well as museums, theaters, restaurants, parks—and, most importantly, the beach.

Annaday was charming, cozy, and romantic—and rumored to be the exact locale of their daughter's conception. Lending further credence to the rumor, Anna Day Hart was born exactly nine months later, back in Iowa...

•

Red's gaze left the photo of Anna's parents and wandered up the cracked plaster wall to the old newspaper clipping that now dangled precariously from a bent thumb tack. Wrinkled, torn, and faded, the article and accompanying photo was a daily reminder of a life now past; a tiny portrait of himself and his beloved wife, their little white cottage home, and the surrounding yard bursting with lavish plants and flowers that they had fostered together.

Red sighed, shaking his head.

Ten years already.

It seemed like only yesterday...

•

The winter of 1995 had lingered a bit too long, drawing the cold days out like a prison sentence. Staying indoors whenever possible, the townsfolk of Mill Springs, Iowa watched out their windows, waiting.

March...April...

Then, one day in late April—better late than never, as they say—a welcomed patch of spring weather finally arrived, and with youthful energy and zeal set about scrubbing the bitter gloom from the day with a brisk warm breeze.

This sudden turn had Red jazzed, like finding a dollar on the sidewalk; so he and Anna eagerly took advantage, heading outdoors to start work on their famous garden paradise.

For years, the happily married couple had cultivated a veritable jungle of plants, flowers, and natural landscaping around their quaint little cottage house. Birds, rabbits, chipmunks, squirrels, and a host of other wildlife thrived in the natural habitat. Their front yard would have given the Garden of Eden a run, and they were inundated with compliments from awe-struck neighbors, visitors, and even casual passers-by.

On a deeper level, they both viewed the rich fecundity of their beautiful homestead as merely a reflection of the health and vitality of their own thriving, fertile marriage; a natural extension of themselves and their undying love for each other, which was perpetually growing, expanding—and sometimes even filling in the details on its own.

Their astounding horticultural success had even landed them a short article in the local community newspaper, *The Mill Springs Messenger*, along with a full-color photo (back then, meriting a color shot in the newspaper was a rarity) as the elderly couple stood, arm in arm, enshrouded in their own rich green elysium, Red beaming and Anna tickled pink.

Next day, Red watched as Anna meticulously clipped the article from the newspaper, and carefully pinned it up beside the big bay window in the dining room, prominently displayed for all to see.

She was so adorable.

Now she threw open all the windows, scurrying about as fresh spring air gently filled the curtains throughout the house. That done, she pulled on her green coveralls and matching gardening gloves, and donned her favorite pink wide-brimmed sun hat. Aptly suited, she then fetched her little garden tool caddy from its winter hibernation in the garage.

As Red set about oiling up the hedge trimmer and mixing a new batch of gas in the garage, Anna went to work in her beloved flower garden out front. Sometimes the breeze carried her faint voice to him, and he could hear her humming complacently along as she plucked weeds, trimmed dead leaves and buds, straightened the occasional errant brick along the edges.

Their neighbors began emerging as the morning progressed, and soon the entire neighborhood was abuzz with an ironic symphony: the mechanized restoration of nature.

The day wore on, and Red was trimming the shrubs around the side of the house when he noticed the afternoon was getting a little warm, the trimmer was getting a little heavy, and he was getting a little thirsty. On impulse, he decided to surprise Anna with a cold glass of iced tea. He slipped inside, careful not to track mud off his work boots as he knocked across the hardwood floor back to the kitchen, then through to the dining room where the sun tea jug was basking warmly on the deep sill of the bay window.

Picking up the jug, he paused to gaze at the *Mill Springs Messenger* article hanging next to the window, and smiled—and noticed it seemed like Anna was actually smiling back at him from the tiny photo. Suddenly giddy, he returned to the kitchen and fixed two tall glasses, dropped in some lemon wedges, and tip-toed the drinks to the front door.

Nearing the door, he noticed that he no longer heard her cheerful humming—and hoped she hadn't heard him coming, the sharp tinkling of the ice cubes against glass blowing his cover. Easing the storm door open, he stepped quietly out onto the front porch and into the warm breeze, smiling ear-to-ear, burning with anticipation; he couldn't wait to see her beautiful face light up with surprise and delight.

He turned to her, and the smile dropped from his face.

The aneurysm had left his beloved Anna face down in the mulch, her petite gloved hand still clutching the tiny shears. Her pink sun hat skipped across the lawn in the breeze, as if trailing Anna's departing soul.

Two ugly brown tea stains permanently sealed the dismal memory into the cement porch where he stood.

•

Anna's Social Security checks stopped coming.

Worse, they hadn't bothered taking out a big life insurance policy on her—they both assumed she'd outlive him—so they got a minimal policy on her, and got a bigger policy on Red.

As it turned out, her tiny policy barely covered the funeral expenses, with just enough left over to buy Red some time to sort things out.

But as time passed, Red struggled. The money was running out pretty quickly, and he realized that he was going to have to sell some of his things if he wanted to keep the house.

After giving it some serious thought, he decided he could part with his motorcycle. Hell, it didn't even run anymore, it was so old. But it was a classic: a '74 Honda Gold Wing, first year they made them. Red had bought it brand new, and he'd zipped all over town on it for years, Anna riding behind, hanging onto him with one hand, and her hat with the other.

Yes, the bike had given him some wonderful memories— but he hadn't ridden it for years. And last time he tried, it wouldn't even start. So there it sat under its cover in the garage, basically useless, just taking up space.

Now who would want to buy that old thing?, as he placed the ad in the local paper. But sure enough, someone did.

Quiet, soft-spoken guy, Red guessed to be in his mid-thirties, with bright blue eyes and shoulder-length sandy-blonde hair. Said he planned to rebuild it from the ground up, then ride it across the country. Said it'd always been a dream of his, and he'd promised himself he'd do it before he was forty, come hell or high water. He'd just been waiting to find the right bike —and here it was. Perfect.

Paid the full asking price in cash, and Red gladly handed over the title and keys, and threw in both his and Anna's helmets. Using some boards Red fished out of his garage, they made a makeshift ramp and rolled the old bike up into the back of the guy's pickup, then shook hands, and that was that.

Red could survive for a little while longer.

But soon, the money was running out again. So, after much lamenting and arguing with himself, he finally decided that he had no choice, he was going to have to sell his prized possession: his silver '64 Ford Mustang convertible, in mint condition —complete with whitewalls, leather seats, dual exhaust, and stock radio. He had restored it himself, by hand. Took him years, but he had to do it, couldn't help himself; after all, he was a ragtop man—just like his dad.

Aside from Anna and their home (and good ol' Max, of course), he cherished that car more than anything else in the world. And now, other than the house, that sleek sliver beauty was all he had left.

With sadness in his heart, he placed the ad.

And just like the Gold Wing, it didn't take long.

Kid took a cab all the way down from De Moines to buy it —a college dropout who'd decided he'd rather spend his trust fund on "a sweet ride" than on finishing college. When the boy showed up—bloodshot and reeking of booze and easy money—Red sadly handed over the title and keys.

Tears welled up as he stood in his driveway watching his beloved automobile pull away, just as he had watched his beloved Anna's sun hat skip away that awful day last summer.

As he watched the car meander up the street and turn the corner, Red felt as if his very soul had gone along for the ride.

But at least he'd bought himself a little more time...

He continued to struggle alone. He tried to keep himself busy working around the house; there was always something needing fixed, or replaced, or simply maintained. Same with the lawn—he worked the lawn daily, but it was getting away from him, growing and weeding up faster than he could trim and cut and pull. And at the same time, he tried his best to keep up the laundry, the cooking and cleaning.

But it wasn't long before he saw the handwriting on the wall. It was simply too much house for just him, too much to take care of alone. He was falling further and further behind. At his age, and in the heat of summer, the lawn maintenance alone was becoming more than he could handle by himself—and, truth be told, even more than what he *wanted* to handle, without Anna there to share it with him.

One day, while on his hands and knees futilely weeding the flower garden out front, he suddenly stopped. Letting out a long sigh, he sat up, wiped the sweat out of his eyes with the back of his arm, then removed his hat and wiped his other arm across his forehead.

Exasperated, he looked up into the sky for a moment, as if beseeching the heavens, then looked back down at the weed-ridden flower garden that lay before him. Turning, he took in the entire landscape behind, all of which was fast becoming overgrown, unkempt.

Anna, I just can't do this anymore, as he glanced around the property, the house, all the work to be done.

And besides, I don't want this without you.

With that, he replaced his hat, sighed in resignation, stood, brushed off his knees, pulled off his gloves, and headed inside for a tall glass of iced tea.

Inside, ice clinking against glass, his forlorn gaze went from the *Messenger* article still hanging next to the big bay window in the dining room to the solemn grave marker out in the back yard, where Max was buried. From where he stood, he could just see the big white rock he had painted himself, his beloved dog's name painted across it in black, nestled behind a cluster of small pines in the back corner of the yard.

Standing there in lonely silence, Red finally came to terms with his situation: he was going to have to give up the house. Realizing this, he wondered what the hell he would do, where the hell he would go.

Mostly, he wondered if Anna would ever forgive him.

Next day, after carefully consulting the *Realtors* section of the Yellow Pages, he made the dreaded call.

•

Upon consulting with the realtor, and having his property appraised, Red learned that the entire area had depreciated in value over the years—and his neighborhood was one of the older ones in the bunch—and he was forced to list his home at considerably less than he thought it would be worth.

On a brighter note, it had sold rather quickly—the relentless upkeep he'd performed since day one, and the veritable garden paradise he and Anna had fostered over the years, prompted a quick sale. The upgrades and renovations, along with the lack of any required repairs, made it very attractive to investors.

In the thirty days he had to vacate, he held several estate sales, and sold off most of his and Anna's possessions, pretty much anything he didn't need on a daily basis. He gave what was left to friends, charity, and his lifelong church, Southern Plains Baptist.

And that was where his old life finally came to an end, and his new life began, living poor and alone in this ancient apartment building in town. After selling his house, by the time he paid off the mortgage, and paid all the costs and fees of selling the house, and paid the movers to move him here, there wasn't much left.

On the advice of Earl Collins—the finance manager at the bank, whom he'd known for decades—he put the paltry remainder of his money in a money market IRA, which paid a good rate and was easily accessible if for some reason he wanted to draw from it, like in case of emergency.

Aside from what little money he socked away in that account, he was now essentially broke, standing silently in this ancient apartment, trying to remember the happy, fulfilling life that was once his...

•

His sad gaze wandered from the newspaper clipping back to the dresser below. There, a stack of old snapshots, wrapped in a rubber band. Removing the band, he silently thumbed though pictures of his son James, taken over the years as he grew out of his britches right before Red's astonished eyes.

Pictures while vacationing on the beach, or camping, or visiting with friends. First day of school, first school play, first bicycle; the ten-year-old boy loaded down with newspapers for the paper route he delivered his last two years of grade school; later, playing french horn in the band in junior high; posing with his first girlfriend Heather; working behind the counter at his first job at Baskin Robbins, his apron smeared with thirty-one different colors of ice cream.

Finally, his high school graduation, after *the change*—you could already see it in his face, staring blankly at the camera, unsmiling, seemingly with contempt. By then, Red and Anna had suspected there was something wrong with the boy—he had dropped out of band, quit his job, become entirely unsocial, no girlfriend, at least that they were aware of—but they didn't know what to do, or how to approach him about it.

But then he went off to college that fall, and that was that. They saw him off at the bus station, a somewhat distant hug for mom, a tentative, no-eye-contact handshake with dad, then he turned and boarded the bus without another word. Red and Anna returned home and hoped for the best.

But it all went downhill from there.

James immediately got caught up with the wrong crowd. Drinking, drugs, partying. He made it through the first semester, barely—then dropped out in the middle of the second.

From there, he went off into his own world, and Red and Anna scarcely heard from him. And whenever they did, he was usually in some kind of trouble. Though he had eventually sworn off the drugs—some close calls with deals gone bad had wised him up, and he finally decided he'd had enough of that scene—his drinking slowly got out of hand.

But over the years, he somehow seemed to make his own way. He worked on and off at a variety of jobs, moved around a lot between cheap apartments and rental rooms—but for the most part seemed to stay out of trouble with the law.

And his relationships suffered in the same way that his jobs and living quarters did: in and out, like a revolving door. He'd even gotten married once, but it ended quickly in divorce.

The only thing that remained consistent in their son's life

was the drinking—and, of course, the many related problems that typically arise from that type of impulsive, irresponsible, destructive lifestyle.

But then one day, things changed, James made a turn for the better—or so they had hoped at the time—and they were willing to do anything they could to help him out, to give him a shot at finally leading a normal, productive life.

So when he came to them asking for their help with a business venture he was interested in pursuing, they were all ears. Anything they could do to help him out.

But now, in hindsight, Red regretted them ever having given him that loan...

•

Years prior, Red and Anna had paid off their original mortgage, and—at least for a short time—owned their little cottage house free and clear. But soon they took out a new mortgage—pulling most of the equity from their home—to loan to their son to start his own business; some sort of pizza franchise that Red was unfamiliar with, but James was extremely excited about.

Evidently, for a "small up-front investment", the company would do all the research to help James find the perfect demographic location, negotiate the lowest possible leasing terms for the property, assist him in securing financing for all the structural remodeling and restaurant equipment (with an additional down payment on each, of course). The parent company also promised to handle all of the local advertising for James, bringing waves of customers streaming through the doors of his very own pizza parlor.

The company all but guaranteed James that he would soon be a successful business owner; all he had to do was come up with the franchise fee and down payments, and they would do all the work for him; then all James would have to do is sit back and rake it in.

Red and Anna were leery, to say the least—but James was relentless, and finally talked them into it. For one, James had always had trouble holding down a job, was perpetually suffering long bouts of unemployment. They were encouraged by the fact that he was finally showing a little motivation, and actually trying to do something with his life. And, during his pre-occupation with this franchise, he had actually sobered up.

For awhile, at least.

So Red and Anna took out a new mortgage on their home and handed the small fortune over to their son, who in turn handed it over to the franchise company.

But it wasn't long before the various fees and down-payments started piling up, along with the cost of licenses, permits, and a host of other unforeseen expenses that were suddenly required. Eventually, that "small up-front investment" grew to nearly $100,000—the entire amount of the loan, of course.

And wouldn't you know, James's new pizza restaurant never materialized; one day, the parent company just up and vanished. James was suddenly receiving harassing phone calls and letters from angry equipment vendors, contractors, property managers, and utility companies, all of whom had wasted their time working up useless quotes, writing up unsigned contracts, vainly calculating production and shipping costs, and getting all the utilities set up and turned on—only to discover the franchise company's phone number was suddenly disconnected. They all then turned to James, who insisted he knew nothing about any of it.

With time, the firestorm faded away, eventually sputtering out with idle threats of legal action. Fortunately for James, it all dissipated to nothing more than a round of negative reports circulating the credit agencies.

But the money was now gone, the business never got off the ground—and James was drinking again.

Meantime, Red and Anna had acquired a brand new house payment, which was difficult for them to make, both being retired and on Social Security. After waiting for quite some time and hearing nothing from James concerning what he intended to do about the loan, Red finally called him and inquired about repayment. To his astonishment, James acted surprised—even offended—that Red had even asked, then proceeded to explain:

"Dad, that money wasn't a *loan*, it was an *investment*—"

investment?

"—and unfortunately, the business didn't pan out like we'd hoped, and so now the money's gone. There's nothing I can do about that."

Then, as if simply shrugging it off: "Sorry."

sorry?

To Red, the flippant attitude with which James conveyed this news was both astounding and disappointing.

Sadly hanging up the phone, he wondered if James truly was born of his own flesh and blood...

•

Wrapping the rubber band back around the stack of photos, he returned them to their place on the dresser beneath the framed collage. As he did so, his eyes came to rest on a handful of glossy, full-color brochures sitting there in a haphazard pile —those evil brochures that he hated looking at with every fiber of his being—and anger swelled inside him as he recalled all the events of the last two days...

•

The prior Thursday, he'd been sitting on his sofa watching a movie on his portable console TV. It was one of Red's all-time favorites: *The Searchers*, a western starring John Wayne and Natalie Wood. It was late morning—approaching noon—and he was getting a little hungry. But about the time he was thinking about fixing a sandwich—maybe next commercial—the phone rang.

Frowning, he looked across the room at the phone sitting on the small table next to his recliner.

Odd...who could that be?

Second ring. Ambling over, he glanced once or twice back at the TV, hoping not to miss anything good.

He picked it up just as it began to ring a third time.

"Hello?"

A woman's voice replied, "Yes, could I speak with a Mr. Kelly, please?"

"Speaking."

"Ah, good. Mr. Kelly?"

"Yes?" He didn't recognize the voice.

"My name is Judith McAlester, I'm with the Social Services division of the Veteran's Administration. How are you doing today, Mr. Kelly?"

"The V.A.?" Red asked. "What's this about?" Suddenly, he got a bad feeling in his gut.

"That's right, the V.A., Social Services division. Mr. Kelly, the reason I'm calling is I've been directed by the department to perform what we call a wellbeing check. It's routine, really, and can usually be resolved via telephone interview. So I'd like to ask you a few questions, see how you're doing, make sure everything is okay. Do you have a minute to answer a few—"

"Of course I'm okay!" he stated sternly. "Why wouldn't I be okay? What's this about? Why are you calling me, out of the blue like this?"

Red was getting angry, and he suspected he knew exactly what the problem was, why they were checking on him...

"Mr. Kelly, please calm down. It's just that we received a call concerning your wellbeing, that's all. I'm calling you to follow up, make sure everything's okay."

"A call? About me? From who?"

"Yes, Mr. Kelly. From a—"

—the sound of papers shuffling in the background—

"—Mr. Woods. Carl Woods. Apparently, he's the—"

"Manager of my apartment building," Red interrupted.

"—yes," she confirmed.

"Yeah, Woods is a real troublemaker, tell you what. Can't ever mind his own damn business. And he called you? Why?"

But Red suspected he already knew.

"Mr. Kelly—"

"Okay, stop with the Mr. Kelly nonsense," he interrupted. "Just call me Red, same's everyone else."

A sigh on the other end, again the sound of papers shuffling.

"Sure,"—

—more papers shuffling—

"—Ted."

"Red."

"Okay. Red then. The initial call was made to the State Health Department, but when they checked your records, and discovered you're a veteran, the case was forwarded to the V.A., and they transfer all such cases to the Social Services division. That's me. I was assigned to your case."

"Case?" Red stated, confused. "What case?"

"*Your* case, Mr. Kelly. The V.A. has opened a routine wellbeing case for you, prompted by the report received from the management of your residential building. The protocol is that first I conduct a telephone interview, get an overall idea of your situation, see how you're doing. Then, if I determine it's necessary, I'll come meet with you in person, ask some further questions, make a more detailed assessment."

"Assessment? But I already told you, I'm fine!"

Ignoring him, she continued: "But if you *are* having problems, any difficulties whatsoever, we can help you, Mr. Kelly. There's lots of ways we can help, things we can do for you, if you have a need. You're a World War II vet, and we take pride in helping all our veterans however we can. We owe you. Our country owes you."

"Okay, then how about you forget all this nonsense, and tell Woods to mind his own damn business?"

"Mr. Woods is concerned about you, that's all. He's your landlord, and he has a right—in fact, a *responsibility*—to make such a call if he feels that any of his tenants are having...(a pause)...*difficulties.*"

"Difficulties? Is that what you call it now?"

"Mr. Kelly—"

"Red."

"Red, it's not at all unusual for veterans of your age to—"

"Become senile? Lose it? Become an invalid? Is that what you're trying to say? If so, I can tell you right here and now that I'm fine. I can take care of myself. In fact, I was doing a pretty good job of it when you called me and interrupted my lunch!"

"Mr. Kelly—Red—it sounds like you're exactly right. And that's what I need to find out. Please calm down..."

"I'm telling you, I'm fine. Do I sound like a driveling idiot?"

"No sir, you don't. But it's my job to find out. Ask the official questions, check the right boxes, turn in the report. Quick and painless. So I'd like to ask you a few questions. Do you mind?"

"I don't *want* to answer your questions. I don't *need* to. I'm tellin you right now, I'm fine!"

"Please, Mr. Kel—Teh—*Red*—the sooner we get this over with, the sooner we can put it behind us, and the sooner the

V.A. can quit worrying about you."

Red thought that sounded a bit pushy. Getting suspicious, he asked: "I don't have a choice, do I?"

"Not really, no—"

—the distant sound of typing on computer keys—

"—we can try to work around your schedule, of course—but in order for you to continue receiving your benefits, we'll need to complete the wellbeing check—which could be satisfied with the phone interview, that's not uncommon—so we can ascertain your condition, go from their. Determine if you still meet the qualifications."

"Qualifications?" Red repeated, incredulous.

"Yes, qualifications. To continue your current level of benefits, or if any adjustments need to be made, or if there's any further assistance we can offer you. And, like I said: the sooner, the better."

Sensing futility, and fearing for his benefits, he relented.

"Fine." he sighed. "If I must."

"Very good, Mr. Kelly," she responded. "I've already put your file together, so we can begin now if you'd like. Nothing hard, shouldn't take more than a few minutes."

"Okay, shoot."

He again heard papers shuffling in the background.

"Now, Mr. Kelly—"

"Red."

"Yes. Red. We'll start with next of kin. Public records show that you have a son?"

"Yes. James."

"Full name James Jefferson Kelly?"

"That's him."

"Okay, I think I've already got his social—"

—papers shuffling—

"—yes, here it is. Now residence. I'm showing an address of 1601 South Arbor, apartment twelve?"

"Sounds right. Last I checked, anyway. Don't hear from him much these days."

"And do you have a current phone number for him?

"I don't think so...like I said, we don't talk much anymore. We had a bit of a falling out some years ago. But I could look around, see if I have it written down somewhere."

"That's okay, Mr. Kelly. There's three phone numbers listed in his public records, and one is less than six months old. I can try those."

This last statement struck him as odd.

"What do you mean, try those?"

"In case I need to contact him for anything, that's all. Do you have any other children?"

"Nope. Just James. He was more than enough."

Okay, then, let's move on to extended family. Do have any other surviving—"

"None." Red bluntly interrupted. "My wife Anna passed on some ten years ago, and obviously both our parents—"

"No siblings? You or your wife?"

"No, no, no," Red answered somewhat forlornly. "I was an only child. Anna was too—in fact, even *she* was unexpected, her parents hadn't planned to have any kids. They say she was an accident, called her a "honeymoon baby"—

—he made air quotes as he said it—

"—and fact is, *she* should have outlived *me*—you should be askin *her* these questions—but the Lord took her home early..."

The questions droned on in this way for about fifteen minutes, and Red answered the best he could manage—some were painful to think about—while he listened to papers shuffling and computer keys clicking on the other end of the line.

Finally, Judy said, "Okay. That's it. See, that wasn't so bad, was it? Quick and painless!"

"So how'd I do? Red ask, grinning at the phone. He thought he'd done all right.

"So far, so good, Mr. Kelly—"

"Red."

"Er, Red. Yes. I'll be using the questionnaire, in conjunction with the original report, to generate an initial case report along with recommendations that I'll be filing with the department head for review, assessment, any approvals needed. While I'm waiting for that—usually takes a few days, sometimes as long as a week—I'll be verifying the rest of your file information, make sure all the contact info we have is accurate and up to date, stuff like that."

"So what happens now?" he asked. "You come for a visit?"

"Mr. Kel—Red—from what I've been able to ascertain from this interview, I'd say that probably won't be necessary. I can coordinate things from here, determine your situational needs —as well as whether you qualify for any further benefits—all based on the information contained in your case file."

"Sounds good!" Red was grinning now.

"Keep in mind, though, that the rest is not up to me, I'll be waiting for the final assessment and any needed approvals from my department supervisor. Meantime, if there are more complaints or reports from your landlord—or anyone else, really—you can bet they'll want me to visit, do a more thorough analysis and report."

"There won't be." Red assured her.

"Good. And if that's the case, I think we should be able to move forward with your case within the next couple weeks—maybe a month tops—without any further investigation."

"So I need to behave myself for a month."

She chuckled.

"Mr. Kelly, I'll be checking back with you via phone within the next week to ten days, make sure everything's going okay. If there are any problems between now and then, I'll probably have to schedule a visit within the next two weeks—which I'd rather not do, it's so much easier if we can handle everything through the system, not have to get so personally involved—so yes, we've got maybe a month to get this all ironed out, make sure everything goes smoothly for you from here."

"It will. You got my word."

"Okay. Excellent. I'll be calling you next week, soon as I hear back from my boss, let you know the next step. Thank you for your time and cooperation, and take care, Mr. Kelly."

"You too," he said as politely as he could, before slamming the receiver down with a *diiiiiing.* "And it's RED!" he hollered at the phone, now sitting idle on the table.

Then, snatching the phone back up to his ear, he punched 0 and waited, fuming. The phone on the other end rang nearly a dozen times before someone finally picked up.

"Front desk," Mr. Woods stated without emotion.

"Woods, you asshole!" Red barked into the phone.

"Oh, I should've known it was you, Kelly. Nobody else lets it ring all damn day like that. Most people have enough sense to know that I'm busy, and to try back later!"

"Don't give me that," Red hissed. "Busy. Hah!"

An impatient sigh. "What do you want, Kelly?"

"I just got a call from some lady at the V.A.—social services somethin or other. She told me you called 'em, and now they're on my ass, wanna meet with me, assess my condition, my... *qualifications*...and they're threatening my benefits! I wanna know why the hell you did that!"

"Mr. Kelly, you're the one who came down here the other

day, yelling, causing a ruckus, and threatening me."

"What? You mean Saturday? I only came down there to get my mail, that's all!"

"We were already closed. I told you that. Office closes at four on Saturday."

"Shit! It was just a few minutes after, and you were still there! Just standing there! You couldn't've just reached behind you, and handed me my mail?"

"Not when the office is closed. You know the rules. And besides, I had other work to do."

"No, you were just being an asshole! There's no reason you couldn't've just handed me my mail!"

"Not after hours, Kelly. It's against the rules. And besides, once you threatened me, I wasn't about to do you any favors."

"Threatened you? I never threatened you!"

"You threatened to club me. Swinging that damn stick of yours all over the place."

"My cane? You know I need that for the stairs down there! And I wasn't threatening you with it, I was just pointing at the stack of mail sitting on the counter behind you! And besides, you're tellin me you're afraid of an old man and his cane?"

"Doesn't matter. Fact is, you were causing problems, you were breaking the rules, and you were threatening me...and besides, it's not the only incident. There are others."

"What others?"

"Complaints."

"Complaints? From who?"

"Other tenants on your hall. Complaints about noise coming from your apartment—your TV blaring, for instance—complaints about bad smells, complaints about you talking to yourself up and down the hallway. You're bothering people, Kelly. And you're worrying people. And I'm not sure I want to continue tolerating it. So I called the state health department, asked them to check up on you. It's company policy, Kelly—I gotta report it to the authorities if I think a tenant is having problems. Especially...well, elderly tenants, no offense. It's not up to me. It's part of my job as Residential Manager."

"Problems? You think it's *me* that's got problems? Shit, these plaster walls are so damn thin you can hear *everybody's* damn TVs! And stereos, too! And bad smells? The whole damn building stinks! Full of bugs, roaches, you name it! You're lucky the health department doesn't come in here and shut the place down! I should call 'em down here myself, have 'em take a look around! And since when is it anybody's damn business if a man talks to himself? Huh? What's so wrong with that?"

"Mr. Kelly, I've got to go, there are people down here I need to tend to. And I can't be tying up the office phone like this. I'll reassess your residency here once I hear back from the V.A.'s office, and we'll—"

Red slammed the phone down. Again.

He turned to the TV just in time to see the credits rolling.

And suddenly, he was no longer hungry.

•

Next evening—Friday—he was sitting in his recliner working a crossword puzzle he'd stumbled across in the morning paper, when the phone rang again. Perplexed, he reached over and answered it, and was astonished to hear his son's voice on the other end, asking him if he could treat his "old man" to dinner, someplace nice, where they could enjoy a few cold ones and "catch up."

Red had not spoken with James for quite some time, and he was more than a little suspicious about him calling out of the blue like that; nevertheless, he reluctantly agreed.

That evening, Red raised his eyebrows when James showed

up actually wearing a decent dinner jacket—though the faint stench of alcohol and cigarette smoke was still detectable even over the overpowering aroma of cheap cologne.

They immediately headed out, and it seemed to Red that James was being somewhat talkative and overly friendly as he drove them to a popular microbrew in town. Once seated, they indulged in random small talk over frosty mugs of beer that left wet rings on the thickly lacquered wood table as they awaited their orders.

Though uneasy at first, soon Red began to relax, and actually started to enjoy the evening with his estranged son.

When the waitress delivered the sizzling steaks, the small talk ceased and they both dug in.

After a few minutes of sawing and chewing, nothing but the din of the busy diner and the distant clanging and muffled hollering back in the kitchen behind the bar, James stopped for a moment, donned a serious look, lowered his voice, and said:

"Look, Red—"

Red?

"—I know you're in a bad way, with Mom gone and all, and that rat-hole of an apartment you've gotten yourself into—"

gotten MYSELF into?

"—especially in that neighborhood. I mean Christ, just look around! The place is crawling with blacks—*and* Mexicans!"

As his son spoke, Red casually sawed at his steak, annoyed.

James pulled a pack of cigarettes from his jacket pocket, shook one to the top, and slid it out with his lips. Unlit, it danced with his words as he starting fishing his lighter from the other pocket.

"Dad, that place is filthy, it's dangerous, and I worry about you all the time." Bringing his hands to his face, he flicked the lighter, covering the flame as he lit up.

Red stabbed a bite of steak, raised the fork up, then paused, shrugging. "I'm fine with it. I served with plenty of blacks during the war. Mexicans too. They're all decent people, just like you or me or anyone else." He pointed the fork back and forth between them as he spoke, then forked the morsel into his mouth.

"Well, that's nice of you to *say*—but I sincerely doubt that you're all that *fine* with it." James looked around again, obviously wary of being overheard, then leaned closer to the table and whispered, "And they sure as hell aren't anything like *us.*"

Red was again disappointed, but not at all surprised; sadly, he had learned a quite a few disappointing things about his son over the years.

James continued: "You're living in a sewer full of riff-raff—" *riff-raff?*

"—and I think we can get you out of that place and into something a lot nicer. I'd like to help you make a...transition."

Hearing this, Red was taken aback; was his son finally going to pay him back some of the money they'd loaned him?

But that word—*transition?* It didn't sit well with him at all. Still somewhat suspicious of this whole event, he put his fork aside and leaned back, took a drink from his mug, thought he'd at least hear what his son had to say.

James pulled one side of his jacket open, reached inside, pulled out a handful of brochures, and fanned them out on the table before Red, spinning them quickly around so Red could read them.

The one on top was entitled *The Golden Years Assisted Living Community: A Home Away From Home.* Red could see that the rest underneath were similar, and he stared at them for only a moment before looking up at James, incredulous.

"You want to put me in a *nursing home?*" he gasped.

"Not a nursing home, an assisted living community. There's a huge difference."

"You brought me out to dinner to tell me you're putting me away? In a *nursing home!?*" His voice was escalating.

"No. Not me, anyway. *I'm* not."

"You're not? Sure as hell looks that way to me!"

Glancing around, James noticed some people at a nearby table had turned and looked at them when they heard Red yelling. He smiled and waved at them, and they went back to their meals. Turning back to Red, he spoke quietly.

"Dad, calm down. Please. People are looking."

"Let them look! Let them watch the heartless son putting his poor old man away!"

James sighed in frustration, shook his head. "Look...the V.A. called me yesterday. A woman named...Judy, I think. Yeah, Judy. She said they're doing some kind of wellness check something or other, that there've been a few complaints about you, and they're concerned."

"She called you?" Suddenly he remembered her mentioning the phone numbers she had listed for James: *I can try those.*

"Yeah, she called me yesterday afternoon, told me what was going on with you."

Red was astounded. Pushing aside his plate, he snatched up his beer mug, took a long drink, then set it gruffly down with a *clunk!*, the beer sloshing side to side.

"So what, exactly, IS going on with me?" he asked sternly. "Last I heard, I was doing just fine. Told her so myself. Just yesterday morning, matter of fact."

James in turn paused to take a swig from his beer before proceeding. Putting down the mug, he stared down at his plate and sighed. Then he looked up.

"Listen...Dad...we both know that you've been struggling,

ever since Mom...you know...since she died."

"I'm gettin along just fine."

"And that roach-infested apartment you're in, and especially in that neighborhood. She told me she ran the demographics, and it's a bad neighborhood, especially for seniors. Especially *white* seniors. That's what she said. And it's not just her opinion, either. It's statistics, based on the demographics, crime reports, the like. She told me that statistically speaking, it's dangerous for you to even be living there. And she said that's what she has to go by when she makes these kinds of determinations. The stats. The numbers."

"Determinations? What determinations?" Red sure didn't like the sound of that.

James paused, took another swig. "That's what I'm trying to tell you. It's not *me*. It's *them*. *They've* determined you need to move, that you'd be better off with a little help on hand when you need it. They gave me some recommendations, so I spent the rest the day running around to all these places—"

—he tapped the stack of brochures on the table—

"—talking to people, gathering all this information for you, so we can pick out the best place for you to move to."

"Move? Don't you mean *transition?*" Red growled.

"Well, yes...transition, if you like. It does sound a lot better, doesn't it?"

Red couldn't believe he actually smiled at him as he said it.

"And the good news is, the V.A. is going to help. The Veteran Housing Program will pick up most of the cost, including the initial move and the bulk of the residency fees. Some of the additional care falls under medical, so that's covered too."

Red sat in silence, still not believing what he was hearing.

James then pulled a folded sheet of paper from his other jacket pocket, yanked a pen from his shirt pocket, unfolded the paper, turned it over, and placed it on the table between them, clicking the pen and setting it on top.

Looking down at it, Red could tell it was some kind of legal form. He looked back up at James, a question on his face.

"What's this?"

"It's called a *durable power of attorney*. All you have to do is sign it."

"Sign it? Power of attorney? What for?"

"Don't worry, I've retained a highly reputable attorney. In fact, you've probably heard of the guy—David R. Jansen? He was on all the talk shows awhile back."

Red frowned.

"Jansen?" He shrugged. "I've never heard of any Jansen."

"Yeah, he worked for that big corporate defense firm, Tanner & Associates, remember? They handled that multi-million dollar lawsuit, Lornes v. Johnson? I'm sure you heard about it, it was all over the news."

Red just shook his head.

"Anyway, the reason this guy got famous is because he quit the case, right in the heat of the court battle. Just up and quit— you don't remember that? Tanner's firm managed to win the case anyway, but they shit-canned Jansen. But then, the story got out why he quit like he did, and ends up he did it for his family. His job was killing him, his marriage was on the rocks, his daughter was becoming estranged, and he decided that his family life was more important than the seven-figure salary he'd make as partner in the firm, so he walked. Well, the media *loved* that—even more than the high-profile case itself—and he made the rounds on all the talk shows. He was even on Oprah."

"I don't remember hearing anything about that," Red said. "But what's he got to do with *this*?" Red tapped on the paper.

"That's what I'm tryin to tell you. Jansen quit corporate defense law after that, and decided to go into wills, trusts, and estates. He wanted to do something that would help other families. So now he does wills, trusts, inheritances, estate transfers, probate, stuff like that—makes it as smooth as possible for the families, keeps the government's hands off as much of it as he can, helps the family retain as much as possible. He's the best in the estate business, and I wanted him to handle ours—"

OURS?

"—so I contacted him, and he's agreed to work with us. He wrote this up—"

—he tapped on the paper between them—

"—and Fedexed it to me. All you have to do is sign it, then I'll mail it back. Then I can handle all your finances from now on—your IRA, your Social Security checks, your V.A. benefits, your medical care, any of your bills not covered by—"

Red didn't hear the rest, because he was already off his chair and ambling across the restaurant toward the front door.

"Dad!" James stood, quickly grabbed up the pen, paper, and brochures, then started after him—but stopped abruptly, setting it all down long enough to yank some cash from his wallet and toss it on the table. Then he grabbed his beer, downed it, snatched everything back up, plucked the burning cigarette from the ashtray, and darted between tables to catch up with Red, who by now was approaching the front doors.

The trip home was wrought with storms of yelling and arguing, interrupted by intermittent bouts of cold silence that, if nothing else, gave them both a chance to catch their breath and prepare for the next round.

At home, Red unlocked his door, stepped quickly through, then turned and slammed it shut in his son's face, turning the lock with a *click!*

Standing there in silence, he watched in amazement as the

shadow on the other side slid the brochures and the legal form underneath, then hollered through the door, muffled:

"Judy said she'll be checking on you over the next couple of weeks! And depending on what she sees, and what she decides —and especially if they receive any more reports or complaints from your building—they'll probably have to move you. So you need to decide where!"

Glaring at the closed door, Red silently flipped him off, then listened as his footfalls faded away down the hallway...

•

Now, as he stood staring at the brochures on his dresser, the paper folded and tucked underneath, he realized that Memory had brought Anger along for a visit—and Red was in no mood for uninvited company. He snatched it all up in a crumple and headed for the trash can in the storage closet.

In the darkness of the closet, Red stomped on the pedal of the trash can, flipping the metal top up with a rattle. He leaned over and stuffed the whole wad in, the crisp crunching of plastic and cellophane beneath music to his ears.

Satisfied, he dropped the lid with a *clump!*

Good riddance, as he brushed his hands briskly together in exaggerated motions, as if ridding them of something foul.

He stood quietly in the darkness for a moment, smiling down at the trash can. As his eyes adjusted to the darkness, his gaze drifted over to the nearly forgotten items leaning against the wall: two faded old collapsible camping chairs; an ancient fishing rod; a bundle of tent poles tied tight with nylon rope.

Seeing them summoned a rush of nostalgia, memories of the good old days when he used to go camping, fishing, or hunting, his loyal companion Max trotting along beside him, barking joyously, tongue lolling and tail wagging as he romped in the wilderness paradise (and Red knew exactly how the dog felt).

On occasion, Anna also went along; to Red, camping in nature with his beloved wife was the closest possible earthly experience to actually being in heaven; after all, as far as he was concerned, she truly was an angel—and those times were, without a doubt, heavenly.

Next to the camping equipment, a rusty flagpole stood leaning into the corner, still wrapped in an American flag; he had removed that from the front of his house when he vacated it. Beneath the rolled-up flag, his trusty Remington double-barrel shotgun leaned, gleaming in the darkness, still shining with the excellent care he had given it all those years.

For a long, silent moment, he stood in the darkness, considering the firearm.

Considering his future.

Considering his options.

Now it was in his hands, still gleaming like a prized trophy. He cracked it expertly open, held it up to the light through the open closet door, and peered into the dark chambers.

Empty. He knew that; he wasn't stupid.

Shells, as he began rummaging through the many items that crowded the shelves. He searched the shelves, his hand darting behind, between, under, around, but finding nothing.

Come on, just one, as his eyes then traveled to the shelves above, which were crowded with even more camping gear: his old tackle box; a cracked, blackened kerosene lantern; a green canteen, its cap hanging off the shelf by a tiny, rusty chain.

Tackle box, as he snatched the plastic case down from the top shelf in a rain of dust, the myriad fishing supplies rattling inside. Setting it atop a tall, rolling travel suitcase stored neatly against the wall, he unsnapped the latches and pulled the top of the box open, tipping it over in the process. A mess of hooks, bobbers, sinkers, and lures spilled out onto the floor before he could right the clattering box.

Should still be here, as he began yanking open the drawers.

Top drawer: plastic boxes of hooks, organized by size.

Middle drawer: sinkers, lures, crimping tool.

Bottom drawer: a few loose hooks mired within a writhe of purple and black rubber worms—and three tarnished shotgun shells stuffed behind them, nearly hidden in the very back of the drawer.

Bingo, as he reached toward the drawer to fetch out a shell.

But he stopped short, arm extended before him, when he suddenly heard muffled shouting start up in the apartment next door. Frowning, he listened intently, staring up at the thin plaster wall that separated the ancient apartments.

It was the man's voice, obviously furious, followed by the sound of something shattering in the distance.

Now the woman was sobbing—possibly pleading—but the man quickly cut her off, yelling even louder now, and the woman stifled a short scream as something once again shattered against a wall somewhere, this time close enough that Red felt the vibrations of debris raining down onto the wood floor through his socked feet.

This wasn't new; he'd heard them argue many times before.

He listened as the shouting next door continued. Then he saw something blink in the darkness beside him just as another *crash!* issued from the adjacent room. Glancing to his right, he noticed a soft circle of yellow light glowing in the corner by the door. He held out his hand, and the circle leapt from the wall to his palm, now smaller, brighter, more defined. As he moved his hand slowly toward the wall in front of him, the circle of light on his palm tightened to a laser-sharp dot.

From there, he followed the rest of the line of travel upward with his eyes, and discovered the source: a tiny hole penetrated the plaster above the breaker box, allowing a nearly invisible trace of light to shine in from the apartment next door.

The cutout for the box was slightly oversized, leaving an open space in the wall above it. Through that open space, the back of the plasterboard next door was visible, pierced through by what was likely a hanging nail driven in from the other side, which had since been removed, leaving the tiny pinhole.

He realized that whatever had been thrown next door had sailed past the pinhole, momentarily blocking the light, thereby causing the tiny circle on the opposite wall to blink off and back on again.

Dropping his hand, he watched as the faded yellow circle re-appeared in the corner by the door.

Suddenly, another loud *crash!* jerked his attention back to the wall in front of him, and to the situation that was apparently unfolding in the apartment on the other side.

Though he'd heard them fight many times before, it had never sounded quite this bad; this time, the man's yelling had greatly escalated, and the woman's sobbing had escalated right along with it.

The situation sounded like it was getting out of hand, but he wasn't sure what he should do about it, if anything. He really didn't want to call the cops; that probably wouldn't make for a good day—or for friendly neighbors afterward, for that matter. And how would it look to Judy McAlester? Surely, she would find out he got into a mix with his neighbors, and the police were called. And hard telling how that asshole Woods would spin things, if given half a chance; after all, he wanted him out of there already.

So getting involved was too risky; he decided he should just mind his own business.

But then, another *crash!* and another scream—both louder

and closer this time—prompted him to reconsider. Should he do anything? It was a really tough call, all things considered.

Finally, he decided he needed a little more information, get a better idea of what, exactly, was going on next door, and what, if anything, he should do about it.

He closed the shotgun, leaned it gently against the wall, then reluctantly crept up to the cutout above the breaker box. Sliding his glasses off, he got up on tiptoes, pressed one side of his forehead to the plaster above the cutout, peered through the tiny pinhole in the other wall with one eye—and gasped.

The man was holding a knife!

It was a big, black-handled kitchen knife of some sort, apparently pulled from the wood block that now lay toppled onto the kitchen counter behind him, with many other knives and kitchen utensils scattered across the countertop and adjacent stove. An upper cabinet door stood open, revealing rows of glasses and stacks of dishes.

The woman was standing with her back to Red, not more than eight feet from the wall through which he was peering. As the man shouted, he waved the knife deliriously with one hand, while reaching up into the cabinet with other, snatching down a glass or dish and flinging it at her each time he came to an accentuated word in his rant.

"I'm the MAN (*crash!*) of this house, and you don't ever question me! If I decide I want to stay out all night, that's EX-ACTLY (*crash!*) what I'll do, and you don't say SHIT!" (*crash!*)

His throws were erratic at best, and the woman—though a large woman and substantially overweight—was able to dodge them fairly easily with a simple duck or side-step; but she was trembling, sniffling, and murmuring pleas for him to stop.

Red stepped back for a moment, frowning as he considered what he should probably do. As he folded his glasses and tucked them into his shirt pocket, an eerie moment of silence ensued next door. Curious, he stepped back up to look, unable to help feeling somewhat like a Peeping Tom.

Peeping Ted, as he peered once again through the pinhole.

Yielding the knife maliciously, the man had moved away from the kitchen counter and closer to the woman. Her arms were crossed around herself as she slowly backed away, moving closer to Red, trembling and sobbing. The man stopped short, looking at something below Red's line of sight. He bent over out of view, then stood and upended a vodka bottle, gulping so fervently that Red could see his Adam's apple bobbing as it stroked the burning liquid down.

My God, as he stood transfixed by the dubious feat.

The man drained the bottle, then flung it at her. This time he was closer to the mark, and she covered her head with both arms as it streaked over her shoulder and across the room. Red flinched away, ducking as the glass missile exploded against the wall that separated them, sending a thin veil of plaster dust swirling about him in the darkness.

Red quickly returned to the peephole—and gasped again.

He was upon her now, jabbing repeatedly, the knife coming within mere inches of her face and neck with each circular lunge. She was slowly backing away, head turned, hands out in defense. As she moved closer to Red, with her head turned to the side, he could now see a cut across her cheekbone, blood smearing into makeup and tears. From that proximity, he could also see blood on her hands—running between her fingers, down her wrists.

Each swing of the blade evoked a small yelp from her through her sobs. Red could barely hear her now, but he had heard enough—seen enough—and now knew that he *had* to do something, and quickly.

This time, he could not stand idly by and allow this to happen, simply because he was afraid for his own wellbeing.

Jaw clenched, he yanked the shotgun from against the wall, then returned to the tackle box. Shoving his hand into the back of the open drawer, he yanked out the three old shotgun shells.

His pulse quickened when she screamed yet again.

He knew he didn't have much time.

Thunder rumbled off in the distance as he turned and exited the closet, absently plucking a rogue fish hook from his finger and tossing it to the floor, where it disappeared with a series of tiny pings.

•

He marched out of the closet and across the room, yanked open his front door, and stepped into the hallway. There he paused, fished his glasses out of his shirt pocket, flipped them open with one hand, and slid them back onto his face.

Then—for the second time that morning—he looked down at his feet.

Socks.

No time for shoes, as he continued forward.

Looking back up, he noticed several heads had appeared through cracked doors down the length of the hallway, like so many prairie dogs peering out in wide-eyed curiosity.

Red walked with purpose toward his neighbor's door, cracking open the shotgun as he went. He didn't even have to look as he slipped the shells inside, one at a time; he'd handled guns all his life—as a veteran soldier, as a lifetime hunter.

It was pure instinct.

He stuffed the remaining shell into his sweater pocket, then slapped the weapon closed, cocked both hammers back, and raised it to his hip. He watched in mild amusement as all those cracked doors slammed shut down the hall *bang! bang! bang!*

bang! like a line of giant dominoes.

He leaned toward his neighbor's door, listening. He heard no sound coming from within. Fearing the worst, he tried the knob—and to his astonishment, it was unlocked.

He quietly eased it open, and looked inside.

The man's back was to him, one arm wrapped around the woman's neck, who was facing Red. Holding her by her hair, forcing her head back, he held the knife close to her soft neck, turning it over and over as he spoke softly to her.

Red entered the room behind him without a sound.

The woman was completely silent now, trembling, following the knife below her chin with wide, terrified eyes. Mascara-stained tears had painted her cheeks in dark rivulets. A smear of blood painted her face from the cut on her cheekbone all the way up and over her ear.

But then, seeing movement by the door, she looked up over the man's shoulder and noticed Red approaching. Eyes widening even further, she gasped.

Following her eyes, the man snapped around, roughly releasing her in the process. She scurried sideways out of reach, then stopped and turned to watch the scene unfold. Hands clamped to her bleeding face, she glanced nervously back and forth between the two men.

The man glared at Red, looking the unexpected intruder up and down in one quick assessment. His eyes stopped on the shotgun, and he actually grinned and nodded as if in approval.

This close, Red saw that the man looked absolutely crazed; dark rings circled his bloodshot eyes, matching the dark wet rings that circled his armpits, soaked through his olive green shirt, which hung open, unbuttoned. The long sleeves were unbuttoned and open as well, dangling haphazardly from his wrists, adding to his unkempt look. Sweat ran down the sides of his face, dripped from his nose and chin; he peered out from under a thick shock of straight dark hair that dangled from his forehead. Red noticed the man was wearing only one slipper, with one bare foot protruding out from under his khaki slacks, oozing blood between the toes where he'd apparently stepped on some broken glass or porcelain, both of which littered much of the floor.

Holding the shotgun at hip level, Red continued forward, pointing the barrel upward at the man's face as he slowly circled him and stepped into the kitchenette.

"Look mister, you can't be abusin your lady like that." His voice was raspy, but firm.

"Whatcha gonna do about it, ol' man? Gonna shoot me? I doubt that—doubt you got the balls—so howzabout you do us both a favor and get the FUCK OUTTA MY HOUSE!" As he screamed the final words, he threw his arm out, pointing the knife at the door that still stood open behind Red. Now he could see that it was a serrated knife, about eight inches long; could do a lot of damage, and quickly.

"Afraid I can't do that, mister," Red said calmly. "Looks like you've done a good bit of damage in here—"

—he motioned around the room with his chin, never taking his eyes, or the gun, off the man—

—and I'm thinkin your lady might be next. In fact, looks like you've already cut her up pretty bad, and I'm not gonna let you hurt her any more. Not if I can help it."

Suddenly the woman piped up in a quiet, shaky voice: "It's okay, mister—Ricky's just pissed off a little, that's all. He's been drinkin, and he gets this way sometimes when he's drinkin. But once he sobers up, sleeps it off, he'll be—"

"SHUT THE FUCK UP!" the man screamed, snapping around and pointing the knife at her. The force of his scream burned his face an angry red, the veins in his temples standing out, glistening with sweat.

She clamped her hands to her mouth, stifling herself.

He turned back to Red. Pointing the knife at Red with one hand, he pointed behind himself with the other, moving his hand back and forth between himself and the woman.

"This here dispute is between me and my wife," the man said calmly, as if being rational now. "It's none of your damn business. It's *nobody's* damn business, cept ours. Mine. So don't you think you should mind your own business, and leave me be to mind mine? Don't you think a man's business with his wife should be private? Specially if she ain't mindin so well?"

"I see a man abusin his wife like that, it *is* my business," Red growled, holding his ground. "I *make* it my business."

The man returned his outstretched arm to his side, a look of disappointment spreading across his face. He looked down and sighed, shaking his head. Then back up to him.

"That's not very neighborly of you...I thought, being a man yourself, you'd understand how it is...and that maybe you'd show me some FUCKING RESPECT, unlike SOME people around here!"

Again, drops of sweat leapt from his nose, his brow, his chin as he yelled.

"Ricky, why don't you just—" the woman started.

"I TOLD YOU TO SHUT THE FUCK UP!!" he cut her off, eyes never leaving Red's.

The two men stood face to face in a long moment of silence.

A clap of thunder roared outside.

Then, to Red's astonishment, the man actually took a step toward him, jaw clenched, eyes darting about. Now only a few feet from the business end of the shotgun, he snapped the knife upward to point it directly into Red's face, the abrupt motion shaking several more droplets of sweat from his face.

This close, Red could smell the booze; the man reeked of it.

Red watched the man closely as he wiped the sleeve of his other arm roughly across his face, blinking the remaining sweat from his eyes. Then, with his outstretched hand, he began turning the knife slowly from side to side, the steel gleaming and glinting in the fluorescent light glowing in the kitchen ceiling above.

His attention drawn to the knife, oscillating in front of the man's olive green shirt, his khaki pants, Red began to feel a little faint, everything suddenly becoming distant. He shook his head vigorously, squinted, tried to focus. But the man began to transform, shape-shift; then everything around him blurred and darkened, every sound becoming like an echo in his head...

As the woman sobbed quietly in the background, the man lowered his voice to a near whisper, and said:

"There'll be lots of land mines tween here and there, too... and snipers...and hell, even friendly fire, been gettin that all over, so many trees and hills and hedgerows—"

—he swung his knife momentarily out and about—

"—can't see shit out there, don't know who or what you're even shootin at half the time—"

—then brought the knife back to Red's face—

"—hate to think a fine young soldier like yourself get shot by a sniper—or, God forbid, friendly fire—and go home in a box... now that'd be a bit of bad luck, wouldn't it...private?"

Red couldn't believe what he was hearing. He again shook his head violently, snapping himself out of it. The sergeant faded and vanished, and it was the drunk neighbor now standing before him, pointing a knife at his face and saying something.

He wasn't sure what the man had just said, but he caught

the tail end of it as he snapped back into the moment:

"...before I send you home in a box..."

The crazed look, the wild eyes, made Red nervous. He had seen that look before, and, just as before, realized that the threat was real. But he also knew that this time, he could—and would—do something about it. That he would not—could not —back down; there was no way in hell he would ever make *that* mistake again.

Resolved, he stared into the man's crazed eyes, unafraid.

"Mister, I'm not goin anywhere. And I'd suggest you drop the knife, right now, and leave the lady be. I don't wanna have to put you down, but God as my witness, I will if I have to."

The man grinned wildly, then growled: "Okay, grampa, let's see whatcha got."

With that, he lunged toward Red, leading with the knife.

The woman screamed.

Red pulled both triggers.

Her scream was cut short by the deafening double-blast.

It had been many years since Red had fired that gun, and the passing time had evidently taken even a bigger toll on his physical strength than he thought. The power of the blast from both barrels caught him off-guard, knocking him back against the kitchen cabinets, where he stumbled along the counter, his free arm flailing behind him, scattering knives and utensils in his desperate quest for purchase.

He nearly went down when he rapped the back of his head on the protruding edge of the range hood, but instead slumped hard against the refrigerator, knocking magnets everywhere. A flock of notes and coupons took flight, fluttering to the floor.

As he finally righted himself, he noticed that single slipper bouncing around on the seat of the recliner, which was rocking back and forth violently and splattered with blood. The knife was spinning slowly in place on the floor in front of the chair.

Squinting through the smoke, Red could not immediately locate the man.

"Oh my GOD!" the woman shrieked at the top of her lungs, as she dashed past the recliner, disappearing behind it. "You SHOT him! OH MY GOD! Ricky! RICKY HONEY!"

Red was both surprised and baffled by the woman's reaction. Perplexed, he stood and watched her, trying to decide what to do next. As the smoke cleared, he finally saw the man's bare, bleeding foot protruding from behind the chair. Crouching over him, the woman began yelling again: "He's DEAD! You shot his whole face off! OH MY GOD!" RICKY! Oh, no, Ricky baby..."

She then trailed off into sobs.

Red walked slowly back to the door. Without turning, he looked up into the hall ceiling for a moment, as if beseeching the heavens, then back to the floor. Turning back to her, he said softly, "I'm sorry, I really am. But he gave me no choice."

"Oh, Ricky...Ricky baby," she whispered through her sobs as she rocked back and forth, cradling her husband's bloody head in her lap.

Red continued: "You should probably call the police."

Looking up at him, she seemed perplexed, as if she didn't understand his words. She was looking *through* him, really.

"Oh, Ricky," she blubbered again, then looked back down. Curling over him, she began sobbing heavily, and resumed her rocking back and forth.

As Red stood looking mournfully down at the poor woman, another crack of thunder issued from above, closer now, this time rattling the windows. And as it rumbled off into the distance, he heard sirens.

Distant, but he knew.

Yes, they had all slammed their doors shut, but they all had telephones. Undoubtedly, the police had already been called, and they were now on their way to the scene of the crime with tires squealing, sirens blaring, and trigger fingers itching.

And Red knew it was over for him.

He lowered the gun to his side, turned slowly, and walked out of the room, head lowered. He could feel all the occupied peep-holes observing him as he shuffled by—but nobody dared open their door as he made his way back to his apartment.

As he entered his apartment, he felt a little queazy; what was once intimately familiar to him now seemed distant and surreal. Leaving the door standing open behind him, he walked across to his favorite reading chair that sat against the opposite wall, under the window, facing the door. lightning flashed outside as he flopped himself into the chair, laid the shotgun across his lap, and sat silently, considered things.

Considering his future.

Considering his options.

Thunder rolled across the sky.

The sirens grew louder.

His apartment was growing dark now, the storm pulling the daylight from the solitary window behind him.

As he sat in the murky darkness, he turned toward the storage closet. The door was still standing open, and, peering into the shadows, he could just make out the silhouette of the trash can lurking within. He thought about the crumpled brochures.

Suddenly, he realized he was now facing not just one, but *two* intolerable futures; that wherever he was going to spend the rest of what in recent years had slowly deteriorated into a worthless, pointless life, it was most definitely *not* going be in this roach-infested apartment. If he had doubted this before, he was sure of it now.

Earlier, he only feared he was doomed to spend the rest of his life in a nursing home; but now, he also feared he could instead spend it in prison. Who knows what story the woman would cook up? She seemed none too happy that her husband was dead now, regardless of the danger he had posed to both of them. He thought of that look she gave him, there at the end. She'd seemed confused, incoherent. Would she cast the blame onto her husband, where it belonged? Or would she cast the blame onto Red?

And then there was Carl Woods, and his reports of complaints from the other tenants, and of Red threatening him. He was probably just *looking* for an excuse to get rid of him...

And Judy McAlester from the V.A. already pretty much thought he was crazy, and it was just a matter of time before they had to put him away...

And of course, James was just itching to sign the papers...

So no, as far as he was concerned, things weren't looking too good for ol' Red Kelly. Earlier, he'd thought spending the rest of his life in a nursing home was unacceptable; but now, it was even worse: instead of a nursing home, he'd likely be spending the rest of his life locked up in prison. Or maybe the nuthouse, who knows? But whatever the case may be, none of them were even remotely unacceptable to him.

Except now, he'd lost his only other option; he'd just spent his last two shells.

As the distant sirens grew closer, he sat quietly, thinking back about his life; his beliefs, his principals, his achievements.

He believed in honor, and duty; he was a soldier, a patriot who had proudly served his country. He believed in character, and integrity; he was a loyal husband to his wife, a fair and generous master to his dog; he was a forthright, God-fearing man, always active in the church, always tithing generously, always doing what he was supposed to do, always doing the right thing.

Always.

So how could this be? How could his life end up this way? After working so hard, all his life, adhering to these important principles in which he so strongly believed—and now *this* was his reward?

Then he recalled that one big mistake—that *sin*—he had committed so long ago, so far away, when he was really just a *teenager*, not even truly a man yet.

So that's why...this is my punishment...this is my hell...

With that, he lowered his chin to his chest, closed his eyes, and wept quietly, the growing wind outside gently buffering the window behind him.

But his sobbing was suddenly interrupted by a loud, hollow rapping sound that echoed up from the wood floor below him. He started, glancing down just in time to see that damn cockroach scurry out from under his chair. He watched through tear-blurred eyes as it fled across the wood floor, pursued by the rolling shotgun shell that had just fallen out of his sweater pocket and onto the floor, stirring the insect from hiding.

As the roach disappeared under the side table, the red and copper cylinder thrummed across the floor in a wide, sweeping arc, stopping a foot or so from the arm of his chair. There it rocked gently back and forth as it settled, silently pointing to him as if he had been chosen for something special.

The miraculous third option, as he reached over the arm of the chair and snatched the shell up from the floor. He'd forgotten all about the extra shell he'd stashed in his pocket on his way to his neighbor's apartment.

Tires squealed on the pavement below his window. The police had arrived, cutting off their sirens as others still wailed in the distance. He knew he didn't have much time as he cracked the barrel and shook the empties out onto the floor.

His front door was still standing open, allowing him to see down the entire length of the hallway. Dozens of tenants had emerged from their dwellings and were congregating at the far end of the hall, by the stairwell. Two blue-clad police officers—one male and one female—suddenly appeared at the top of the stairs, and stopped to inquire of the crowd. They listened intently as an old lady clad in a bathrobe and curlers gesticulated wildly then pointed down the hallway toward his door.

Load...slap...cock...lift...

The officers pulled their pistols and hurried down the hallway toward him, the man taking the lead, the woman close behind. They stopped momentarily at his neighbor's open door, glanced around inside, asked the woman if she was okay, then nodded in response before continuing toward him, moving slowly toward his door, guns outstretched, looking blankly into the dark room, pointing their weapons into the air above him. Apparently, they had not yet seen him sitting across the room in the darkness.

Slowly, quietly, he raised the shotgun.

The oily steel was still slightly warm, and tasted of smoke and flame. Holding the fore-end with one hand and stretching the other out awkwardly, Red could just reach the trigger with his thumb while keeping both barrels wedged into his mouth.

As the officers approached, the man in front finally spotted him, and immediately understood what was he was doing. He began frantically waving his free hand and shouting "Hey-hey-HEY-HEY—"

Red closed his eyes as a solitary tear ran down his cheek.

Anna, I'm coming, as he pushed the trigger with his thumb.

Over the years, Red had fired that shotgun countless times

—hunting, skeet shooting, the firing range, holiday festivities, wedding celebrations, you name it—and, he took meticulous care of the weapon; the Army had taught him that.

And in all that time, it had never misfired.

Ever.

So it took him by surprise when he felt the click of the hammer, but heard only a short, sharp *crack!*, the report having no more potency than a small firecracker—cut short, incomplete.

Opening his eyes, he saw a ring of smoke floating around the chamber. The barrel had jerked slightly in his hand, but that was all; there was no deafening blast, no pain; no escape that he so longed for. His heart sank with a mixture of futility and incredulity, and he no longer had the strength—or the will —to continue on; he collapsed, sliding from the chair to the floor, the gun clattering down beside him.

Looking up, he saw the two officers standing there in the doorway, staring at him, guns relaxed at their sides, eyes wide, mouths agape.

For a long moment all was silent—then a blast of thunder rumbled above, seemingly shaking the room back to life.

As he lay there watching the officers approach, strangely unable to move—it occurred to him that over the last ten years he had somehow become a mere spectator of his own life; he seemed helpless to alter his own fate, to avoid his own demise, to manifest anything positive in his life whatsoever.

So, at that moment, he finally gave up.

He completely relinquished all control of his life, resigning himself instead to just stepping back and watching what happened next. From here on out he would simply accept his life as it unfolded before him, let the chips fall where they may, and then deal with the rewards or the consequences.

So now, resolved to being merely a spectator, he just lay

there and watched.

But what he saw next was not at all what he expected.

The officers holstered their guns, and the woman ran up to him while the man spoke rapidly into the radio on his shoulder.

Perplexed, Red watched as the woman crouched over him and placed two fingers on his neck, feeling for a pulse—but her partner was already shaking his head. He motioned to the window behind the chair with his chin.

"Forget it, he's gone. Most of his brains are up there, on the window."

Red watched the woman glance up behind him and cringe, just as a flash of lightning burned her face a stark white.

"Jes—" her whisper was cut off by a roar of thunder. Shaking her head, she dropped her hand from Red's neck.

The words and actions of the officers were confusing him as he turned his attention to the hallway. The crowd of curious tenants had moved away from the stairwell and clustered around the two apartments on this end of the hall, gasping and murmuring and pointing.

Behind them, two more officers arrived, and the crowd parted to allow them access to the neighboring apartment. Drawing their guns, they instructed the tenants to get back, then disappeared inside.

What Red saw next confounded him even more: the man next door emerged slowly from the very doorway that the officers had just rushed through. His clothing was sprayed with blood—but the flesh of his face was completely intact.

He stopped and stood barefoot among the spectators in the hallway—but nobody seemed to notice him.

Red was scanning the crowd, seeking a reaction—any reaction at all—to the bloody man who now stood seemingly undetected in their midst, when a sudden movement within his own apartment caught the corner of his eye, and he turned to his left, looking toward his bed. A woman was standing there, in front of the dresser, a mere silhouette among the shadows. He squinted, trying to see her more clearly in the darkness.

Anna? as his eyes widened in disbelief.

Anna had always been a lovely woman—clear up to the day she died, at the relatively young age of sixty-seven—but standing before him now, she was as young and beautiful as the day they had met, over half a century ago. Red was astounded; Anna had not aged—not a single year!

She was pretty as pretty could be.

My God, she's beautiful, as he gazed upon her and felt his heart tingle, as it always did, every single time he looked at her. He wanted to speak, but was unable; he was strangely breathless, and could not muster a single word.

As Red gazed upon his beloved Anna, a rapid series of bright lightning flashes outside suddenly strobed the room through the window above him.

With each quick flash, Anna's image all but vanished, then reappeared somewhat translucently in the moments between each burst of light. Astonished, Red caught glimpses of the dresser and the collage of photos on the wall behind her; *through* her.

While thunder roared through the apartment, Anna's image once again solidified, appearing fully opaque in the twilight of the room. She gazed lovingly down upon him, and Red suddenly heard her soft voice inside his head:

Oh Ted, what have you gotten yourself into this time?

Now he knew without any doubt that it truly was Anna standing in the shadows, for only she used his given name of Ted—not Red, as all his friends and co-workers called him. He had acquired that nickname as a child, in recognition of his thick, dark red hair. But Anna—and only Anna—continued to call him Ted. He always loved hearing her speak his true name —it always made him feel so special, so loved—and hearing it once again made his heart leap. But seeing his young, beautiful wife now—and hearing her lovely voice—also filled him with questions.

His eyes beseeched her:

How did you get here? Where did you come from? What's happening?

But his questions remained mere thoughts, his sudden inability to speak frustrating him. But to his surprise, she answered him anyway, again without physically speaking; she simply gazed into his eyes, and he heard her voice in his head:

I've been waiting for you, Ted. Waiting for a long, long time. It's beautiful where I've been—and it will be perfect once you're there with me. We will finally have our own true Garden of Eden. Our own Paradise. So I've been waiting for you, my love...all these years...

Tears welled up in his eyes as he listened to his wife's angelic words. But sudden movement out in the hall once again caught his attention, and he turned back just in time to see his blood-splattered neighbor begin writhing and turning black, multiple dark patches suddenly appearing and growing all over his body, emitting more and more smoke as they spread. Then he threw up his arms and burst into flames, silently flailing as the flames fully engulfed him and he slowly sank downward and disappeared into the floor.

Seeing that the crowd was still completely oblivious to what had just happened in their midst, Red turned back to Anna, perplexed. Understanding the question in his eyes, she smiled, and he again heard her soft, gentle voice speaking to him in his head:

She truly loved him, Ted—but you were right, he was hurting her, he was bad for her, he was threatening her life—and not just today, but many times in the past, too. So this time, you did the right thing. You ended it. Ended her pain, her suffering. And you most likely saved her life. And even though she's upset right now, she'll eventually understand that you were her hero today, Ted. Just like you've always been my hero...

Catching what she had said, he thought: *This time?*

Yes, this time. I know about it now. What happened when you were really just a boy. But in a way, I always knew. I knew there was something, deep in your heart, that you were keeping hidden away, buried from view, even from thought, for all those years. But I let it go, didn't pry. You were a good man, Ted. Good to me, good to God, good to everyone. Always doing the right thing, the just thing, the moral thing, always sacrificing yourself, putting everyone else first. So I figured if there was something from your past that you felt you needed to hide—anything at all—you would either reveal it to me eventually, when you were ready, or I'd allow you to keep that one thing to yourself. You deserved something of your own, something you didn't have to share with anyone else, not even me. But now I know, and I understand. I don't blame you, and I'm certainly not disappointed in you. Nobody's perfect, Ted—but I've always believed you were the closest any mortal man ever could be. And I've seen perfection, Ted—paradise, a place of pure joy—but I simply could not picture being there without you. Without you, it is no picture for me. So I've been waiting for you; I don't want it without you...

Smiling at him as she conveyed these thoughts, her young, beautiful form began to brighten and intensify, becoming radiant in the near-darkness.

Turning back, he looked up at the officers now standing

over him, looking down at the him. The man turned to the woman, and said:

"Let's get an ID, then tape the scene off before the press gets here. If we hurry, maybe we can get outta here before we're stuck making statements all damn night."

His partner nodded, and they separated and kneeled down on either side of him. As they began roughly searching through his pockets, Red began to understand what was happening. He turned back to Anna, and again heard her voice whispering in his head:

Let's go, Ted—it's time to come home.

Although he was unable to move physically, he seemed to rise easily from the floor—a thought more than a motion—and float effortlessly toward his beloved Anna. As he approached, she smiled up at him, her face glowing with love.

I always did love your gorgeous hair, as she reached up and ran her hand through Red's thick hair.

Turning and looking back, he saw himself still lying on the floor in a pool of his own blood, the shotgun lying by his side, the window behind him splashed with red, dotted with pink clumps. The officers were collecting various personal items from all his pockets, tossing them into a haphazard pile on his body's chest.

Alarmed by the bloody scene, Red jerked his hand to the back of his head—but found no injury there now. He relaxed, and exhaled in relief.

He was all there.

But then he realized his hand was feeling an abundance of thick, soft, healthy hair, rather than the course, thinning white hair he'd gotten accustomed to over the last few decades. To confirm what he thought he was feeling, he glanced up into the mirror on the wall behind Anna—and was taken aback.

They cast no reflections in the silver glass.

Several emergency vehicles now idled below his window, their strobing lights pulsing his apartment in brilliant, colorful flashes—and Red looked at the walls all around them.

They cast no shadows upon the walls, either.

The place was now filling with police officers, speaking briskly to one another, talking on radios, and stringing yellow tape about, the crowd of whispering spectators looking on.

Out in the hallway, two officers began taking statements from the crowd, looking for any eyewitnesses. Inside the apartment, the male officer, crouched beside Red's body, turned and watched the action out in the hallway for a moment. Judging by all the pointing, gesticulating, and squabbling, he suspected that a variety of different obscure, confused, and inconsistent versions of the event would emerge.

They always did.

Turning back, he noticed his partner had stopped working and was staring back over her shoulder toward the bed and dresser on the other side of the apartment.

He glanced behind her into the darkness of the room, then back to her. "What's wrong?"

She shrugged. "Don't know. Just got this strange feeling, like someone was back there, watching us. It was really weird."

They locked eyes, and, seeing that she was genuinely disturbed, he again looked behind her, scanned the room, then back to her.

"There's nobody there," he said quickly, turning his attention back to the work at hand.

As Red turned back to Anna, all the noise and chaos in the room began to dissipate, fading into the background as his heart swelled with love and his soul began to heal. Red and his beloved wife held hands, turned from the scene, and floated away, through the wall, out of the building, into the sky, and toward The Light.

Suddenly chilled, the woman officer shivered, and began vigorously rubbing her own arms, calming her sudden goosebumps. She flipped the hair from her face with a quick jerk of her head and looked upward, glancing around at the ceiling above them.

"So cold all of a sudden...where's that draft coming from?"

Her partner stood, leafing through Red's wallet. Looking back down at her, he shrugged.

"It's an old building. There's drafts all over." With that, he pulled Red's driver's license out of his wallet, then tossed the wallet onto the old man's lifeless chest with the other odds and ends they had scrounged from his pockets.

"Here's his ID. C'mon, let's go."

She stood and followed him out, but stopped abruptly in the doorway, turned, and peered once more into the depths of the room, looking all about. All was quiet, just the rain pelting the small window.

"Hmph," she grunted, shaking her head as she left the room.

•

In mere moments the earth was but a tiny speck far out in the blackness of space behind them, and they were now immersed in The Light—a warm, palpable, calming, embracing light of nearly unimaginable brilliance. It actually felt *alive*; a living entity that they were both now a part of, connected to.

A singularity of all.

Immense love and happiness filled Red's very soul, and for the first time in years he felt whole again.

For the first time in years, he was all there.

Anna turned to Red, smiling up at him as their separate forms began to meld together, become one. With pure ecstasy he realized that he would now be permanently re-united with his lovely Anna, never to be separated again. His soul was finally complete as it joined with that of his cherished wife—his one and only true love, his soulmate—and that he would be one with her, forever.

Forever Anna Day.